Planez 2
Written By: Mariah James

PRESS 3SEVE17EEN
PUBLISHING

Press 3 Seventeen Publishing
P.O. Box 30133
Rochester, NY 14603

ISBN: 0-9977252-1-4
ISBN-13: 978-0-9977252-1-6

This is a work of fiction. Any reference of similarities to actual events, real people, living, or dead, or to real locales are intended to give the novel a sense of reality. Any similarity in names, characters, places, and incidents is entirely coincidental.

CHAPTER 1

As told by Malcolm

I was in complete shock to open the door and see Essence's beautiful face. I was even more stunned to see her with tons of luggage. She stood in front of me, with a bright glow. Even in this December weather, my body heated up at the sight of her.

"Honey, I'm home." She cooed before attempting to shy away, but she couldn't hide her gorgeous smile from me.

"Home?" I questioned. I wanted to be sure I heard her correctly.

She gazed into my eyes without saying

a word. Her continuous smile gave me confirmation. Essence strutted her fine ass past me as I dragged her bags in behind her.

I shut the door behind us and took Essence into my arms. Our lips locked as our tongues twirled with each other. My eyes closed as I listened to the soft moans she let out. My hands moved down to her voluptuous ass. Essence didn't have on any underwear; I could tell through her blue jeans. She was infamous for that. I didn't always agree with it, but now I was grateful. I unzipped her pea coat, as she unbuttoned my shirt.

Essence bit her bottom lip as her fingertips traced my built physique. I continued to undress her, wasting no time in between garments. I wanted to spend more time taking care of her body's wants.

"I love you Malcolm." She whispered. Essence had no problem showing me she loved me, but hearing those three words spill from her lips did something to me each time. My entire body felt the vibrations of her passion-filled voice, feeding my soul.

"I love you more." I responded. It was the truth. The love I had for her was more than I could ever imagine loving someone. Aunt Carol and Mama were the only women I have ever loved. Now, I could share this love in an intimate fashion. I was beyond blessed for Essence, for showing me that love does exist.

I yearned to taste Essence now and not a minute longer. I dropped down to my knees and parted her legs. Essence's back touched the front door as her right leg draped over my shoulder. Her pussy was already dripping and the taste was as sweet as a ripened honey dew.

"Ooh baby." Essence's quiet moans grew louder, filling out my spacious foyer. Essence gripped my head, motivating my tongue to showcase a greater performance. She could barely stand as I entered two fingers inside her. Essence stood on her tippy toes, straining to remain balanced on her left foot.

"Mal…." she screamed. Her screams gave me inspiration to move my fingers in and out a little bit faster. I felt her walls tighten up, but it didn't stop me. Soon enough she had exploded in my mouth. Her legs wobbled as she finally lost her balance. I picked her up before she hit the floor and she wrapped her legs around my waist. Essence kissed her juices off my lips.

I proceeded to carry Essence into the dining room to lay her across the table. That first course was just a tease, now I was ready for the main dish. Before Essence could even recover, I was face first in her sweetness again. This time I took my time, making sure my tongue touched every sensitive spot.

I loved the way Essence's legs tensed up as she was building towards yet another climax. When she reached her peak, her legs shook uncontrollably. A smile spread across my face, adding definition to my dimples. My mission was to please Essence. I was a firm believer in letting her get hers, before I got mine.

"I can't take anymore." She called out, but her body said differently. Her body was calling for me and I was sure to answer. That was the beauty in the way we made love. Our connection ran deeper than our bodies could take us.

"Oh, Malcolm." She continued as I slowed down my rhythm. Essence attempted to push my head away, but I pulled in closer. My face was covered and I enjoyed every minute of it.

I slowly entered Essence, stroking her carefully. I made love to her. I wanted to thank her for deciding to be with me, here in Chicago.

As told by Essence

Malcolm made it so hard for me to control myself. I climaxed repeatedly. Just when I thought he was done, he filled me up with his dick. He took his time, just as precisely as he ate my pussy. As he continued to make love to me, I smiled. I was in bliss thinking of the nights to come, where this would be our routine. I was ready to mark every room in this house.

"I'm cumin', baby." Malcolm belched out. He grew larger inside of me, speeding up his pace.

"Let me taste you." I whispered. I sat up on the dining room table and took him into my mouth.

"Oohhhh." He released and I continued to suck as he guided my head. Malcolm succeeded in pleasing me so I did the same.

I got up early the next morning to make us breakfast. Today is my first official day working in Chicago. I was a little nervous, but ready to get started. I hadn't touched a thing that had anything to do with *Jo Nova* in a while, but it was time. Time to leave New York in the past and build my new profound life in Chicago with Malcolm.

"Damn, baby that smells good." Malcolm complimented the delicious aroma that was in the air. He came behind me and kissed my neck. I could feel his morning wood on my ass.

"Why are you dressed so early?" Malcolm asked as he bit into a turkey sausage.

I haven't had time to fill Malcolm in on anything job related, after a night like last night it didn't even cross my mind.

"I'm going to work!"

"Work? You just got here." Malcolm pouted, sounding disappointed.

"I know, but Vincent needs me to start today. We have a lot of things to go over."

Malcolm smirked at me, showing his perfect white teeth. I knew it turned him on to hear me talk about business, he loved when I was in boss lady mode.

"Oh no, Malcolm. Don't get any ideas," I laughed, "C'mon let's eat." I motioned Malcolm to have a seat at the breakfast nook and we devoured our food.

"I can get use to this." Malcolm broke the silence as he licked the syrup off his fingers.

"You better," I winked. I started to put our plates in the sink and wash them.

"Oh no baby. I got this," Malcolm stepped in. "Go ahead and get to work."

I kissed Malcolm on the lips and watched him do the dishes.

"Aren't you going to take me?" I asked, confused. How did he expect me to make it to work without a car?

"Nope!" Malcolm smiled, "you can take one of the cars. Whichever one you like. I'm off today, no driving for me." It was Malcolm's turn to wink at me.

The perks of being your own boss. I'm going to miss that aspect of it. Although *Jo Nova* is still mine, I will have to run a few things by Vincent.

My stomach was in knots the entire ride down to the office in Malcolm's red Audi Q7. I pulled into *Jackson & Jackson's* parking lot. I double checked the address as if I had never been here before. The huge yellow lettering on the front of the building was another dead giveaway, but my nerves were getting the best of me.

"Calm down Essence. You got this." I spoke to myself as I got out the car and walked into the building.

"Welcome to *Jackson & Jackson!*" A beautiful, tall and slender woman greeted me.

"I'm Es…" I began.

"Essence Brown," she finished, "I'm Latifah Washington, nice to finally meet you." Latifah reached out her hand for me to shake. She was very proud and bubbly, nothing like Shanell. The thought of Shanell made me sweat.

"Are you okay, dear?" Latifah asked. I was unaware that my demeanor had changed.

"Me?" I stumbled, "yes, yes. I'm fine."

"There's nothing to worry about Essence. I've seen your work and here at *Jackson & Jackson* we only have the best!" She nudged me and continued to walk ahead. I followed behind her scoping out everything. The atmosphere had a different feel than *Jo Nova*, for sure.

"Essence!" A familiar voice called out. I turned around to face Vincent, who too had a huge smile on his face.

"Thanks, Latifah. I'll take it from here." Vincent spoke to Latifah. She waved at me as she took her place back at her desk.

"Latifah is our administrative assistant. She keeps this place in check. You need help with anything, she's your go to girl." I just shook my head. Vincent continued to talk as he gave me a tour.

"And this here is your office." When we reached my office, I was pleased. The space was huge.

"Oh, wow." I sighed as I looked around in amazement.

"You like?" Vincent asked, as if my loss for words, wasn't telling enough.

"Like? Vincent, I love it!" I exclaimed. I was so excited I hugged him. Vincent didn't mind at all, he welcomed my embrace.

"Sorry." I apologized, a little embarrassed. He just smiled.

"So, I'll let you get comfortable, today. But tomorrow. We will get down to business." Vincent rubbed his hands together and walked out of my office. I jumped for joy and spun around my spacious new office. I had so many ideas of how I wanted to decorate it. I couldn't wait to get started. The view was also impeccable, I had a perfect view of downtown Chicago. It reminded me so much of home.

KNOCK. KNOCK. The knock at the door broke me out of my daydream.

"Come in." I sang and Latifah walked in and shut the door.

"Nice view, isn't it?" Latifah asked.

"It's amazing." I was still in awe.

"Much like the city?" Latifah asked. We stood in silence for a bit. I couldn't find myself to answer. Latifah was unaware of the memories I was trying to suppress.

"Well," Latifah kept the conversation going, "I'm here if you need anything. And I do mean anything." Latifah stared into my eyes, as I locked into hers.

"Th..thanks." I stuttered. Our little stare down made me a little uneasy. Latifah smiled as she turned to walk out.

I watched Latifah sashay out of my office. Her confidence spoke volumes. She held her head up high as she walked. She was indeed beautiful with her dark brown skin and slender frame. Her hair was cut low with small natural curls. Her hair had a hint of burgundy that matched her silk smooth complexion. She wore a peach skin-tight dress. Although she didn't have much curves, her ass poked out enough to give it a wow factor. Latifah was fine as hell. I had to reevaluate myself for checking out this woman, but I wasn't ashamed to salute another fine woman, though.

I brushed off the thoughts of Latifah and called to check in with Malcolm.

"Hey baby. How's day one?" Malcolm asked before I could even say hello.

"It's fine baby. Everyone is so nice.

My office is huge! Vincent said I can just take the day to soak everything all in and tomorrow is when the fun starts."

"That's dope! I'm glad today is going fine." Malcolm sounded just as happy as I was.

"What have you been getting into today?" I asked.

"Nothing much. Just cleaning up a bit, you know, nothing major." Malcolm rambled.

"Okay, well you keep doing them non-major things." I responded sarcastically.

Malcolm laughed, "I love you girl."

"I love you too!" I cooed back.

"See you later baby." Malcolm exclaimed.

"See ya!" We hung up the phone. I couldn't help but think Malcolm had something up his sleeve.

"Essence you have a delivery." Latifah blared out through the phone's intercom.

I went out to the front to find a dozen

pink roses waiting for me. I smiled as I thought of Malcolm. I knew he was up to something. I looked for a note. It read:

Baby, I'm sure you're rocking today.
Can't wait to see you later.
I miss you.
Malcolm XOXO

My smile grew bigger at Malcolm's kind gesture.

"Well someone's in love." Latifah interrupted. I looked up to her and her smile, surprisingly, matched mine.

"Yes." I picked up the roses and walked back to my office. I could feel Latifah watching me, my stomach fluttered with butterflies as I hurried along.

CHAPTER 2

As told by Malcolm

"Wassup, my G." Terrance greeted me as I walked into our office.

"Nothin' much, my G. Wassup?" I greeted him back. It's been a while since we've seen each other. Essence moving down hit me so suddenly, so I took a few days off to make sure she was straight.

"Ain't shit. How's my sis?" The way Terrance checked for Essence, I knew I made the right choice. Terrance treated Essence like she was family and that meant a lot to me. I was thankful for their bond.

"She's good, man. Life's good. I'm glad we don't have to take them damn planes back and forth to see each other." Terrance and I both laughed.

"Yeah. I'm sure." Terrance laughed a little longer.

"Iight, jokes over," I pushed him playfully. "Did Walt mention anything about the final meeting for Jones Place?' I asked Terrance.

It was a relief to know we had finally sealed the deal. All the time we spent negotiating was finally paying off. Jones Place was the projects where Terrance and I first met and where a lot of our childhood memories were formed. I wanted nothing more than for the kids to have better memories. The kids in our community needed it. Although times have changed, the struggle is still real. I want the children of Jones Place to be proud to say where they are from and not embarrassed.

Not everyone from our hood were lucky enough to make it out. We were the exception. Some cats who made it out, never came back, but I was not going out like that. Jones Place made me who I was today.

"I handled it." Terrance's work ethic kept my stress level down a ton. I wasn't looking to meet with Walt again. He was a sellout. We fought so hard to keep Jones Place, while all he wanted to do was sell it to some rich white folks that were ready to tear it down and build some bullshit ass mall; nothing that neighborhood needed.

"I don't even know why I asked." I responded saluting Terrance.

"We gotta celebrate bro." Terrance suggested.

"No doubt. Meet me at the crib around 11."

"Bet." Terrance and I dabbed each other up to seal the deal. We spent the rest of the day going over plans, setting up architect connects and getting other things in order. I was looking forward to celebrating tonight and my baby Essence has been working so hard, she deserves to enjoy herself too.

"Hey baby." I greeted Essence when I walked in the door, she paid me no mind. She was too busy with her face in her laptop. Her hair was pulled back, she was wearing her glasses and I knew that meant business. But it was Friday and all that *Jo Nova, Jackson & Jackson* stuff could wait.

"Hey baby!" I said a little louder causing Essence to jump.

"Damn Malcolm! You scared me, I didn't even hear you come in. How was work?"

"I see, you're so busy working. Work was good. So good, we're going out to celebrate."

"Tonight?"

"Tonight." I confirmed.

"But, I have so much to do, deadlines to meet. Vince…" I placed my fingers to her lips, and ceased her rambling.

"Terrance is meeting us here at 11, make sure your fine ass is ready."

Essence drew her bottom lip into her mouth. There weren't many times I had to be stern with her, but I could always tell when I did, it turned her on.

"Okay, Zaddy." She responded and we both laughed.

Essence was taking her time to get ready, but Terrance was late, as usual. So, I didn't even trip. The nightlife wasn't really popping until after 12 anyway, so we weren't missing a thing.

"Essence, you ain't done yet? Terrance is here." I called up to Essence.

"I'm coming, dang." Essence yelled back. She strutted down the steps in a little black dress. The dress was crisscrossed at the top, showing just a little cleavage, tight at the waist and it flared at the bottom. Her dark chocolate legs were lathered up real nice with coconut oil and her pretty pedicured toes were sitting high in a pair of black tied up stilettos.

"You look amazing." I was practically drooling over Essence's beauty.

"Thank you! Mr. Hill you're looking pretty handsome yourself." Essence came close to me, kissing me on the lips.

"Um, um." Terrance cleared his throat.

"My bad, bro." Essence laughed, "you're looking mighty sharp." Terrance blushed, showing his gold grill as he straightened the collar of his polo shirt.

"You know, I do what I can." Terrance bragged. We all shared a laugh as we exited the house.

Terrance suggested we check out a new spot, Stone, in downtown Chicago.

It was real thick inside. Everybody was dressed to a 'T'. Fellas jewelry was shining. You could always tell who had the money and who pretended to have it. Of course, the niggas flaunting the gold chains and wrist watches were swarmed with women. The real ballers stood around, scoping out the scenery. The ladies came out looking good, but my baby Essence had them all beat. I dare a nigga to try her.

"This is nice." Essence screamed over the music as she swayed to the DJ's mix. I nodded my head to agree. I wasn't much of a dancer, a good 2-step was good enough for me, but when Essence started grinding her ass on me, I became a professional; couldn't nobody tell me my moves weren't good.

Terrance got lost in the crowd. He wasn't one to stand around, he had to keep moving. It was cool though. He was fully capable of handling himself. He didn't drink like that either, so I had no worries about him getting wasted and acting foolish. He was somewhere mackin' on somebody's girl.

Essence and I were enjoying our time, when we were interrupted by some tall chick.

"Well, hello there beautiful." She spoke to Essence.

"Hey Latifah." Essence called out, "what are you doing in here?"

Latifah laughed, "the same thing you are doing. Getting my party on." Latifah rotated her hips as she spoke.

"Latifah, this is my boyfriend Malcolm. Malcolm, Latifah works at *Jackson & Jackson*."

"Nice to meet you." I stretched out my hand to shake hers. Her hand shake was firm as she gazed into my eyes.

"You too. I've heard so many great things about you." Latifah winked at Essence causing her to blush.

"Oh really?" I smiled at them both. Soon Terrance was back.

"Hello Miss. I'm Terrance." He took it upon himself to introduce himself to Latifah.

"Latifah." She smiled.

"Latifah." Terrance whispered, "you sure are sexy."

"Why thank you." Latifah's strong confidence grew greater at Terrance's compliment.

"Terrance is Malcolm's best friend. He's such a great guy. You two should go talk." Essence suggested to Latifah. She shot a look at Essence, but she soon put back on her smile and took Terrance's hand. Terrance guided Latifah over to the bar to talk. Terrance looked back at us cheesing from ear to ear.

"She seems nice." I said to Essence.

Essence seemed a little dazed, "Yeah, yeah. She is nice. She's the go to girl at work. She is phenomenal."

"Not better than you." I moved closer to kiss Essence and we shared a passionate kiss.

"Oh baby! This is my song." Essence screeched, pulling me into the middle of the dance floor. I couldn't resist, so I followed her lead.

Essence's body moved so swift to the reggae beat, I felt my dick harden. I could not wait to go home and undress her. My eyes stayed glued to her. I knew everyone around her was being hypnotized because the trance she had me in was crazy.

As told by Essence

Malcolm wasn't much of a dancer, but I appreciated him coming out on the dance floor to dance with me. I'm glad he made me put down all that work crap. It's only been a few short weeks and I was pulling all-nighters, like crazy. I was shocked to see Latifah here. She didn't strike me as a club girl, although she did have this mystery about her. I'm sure that's what drew Terrance into her; including her beauty and the bad ass jumpsuit she was wearing.

I turned my back to Malcolm, as I whined on him. I could feel his hard dick. My pussy trickled at the feel of it. I glanced over at Terrance and Latifah at the bar. Terrance was leaned in close to her ear, spitting game. She didn't seem to be moved by what he was saying; every so often she would nod her head or chuckle. She sat on the bar stool with her long legs crossed watching me. She admired me without blinking or taking her eyes off me.

"Okay, baby. I think I had enough dancing." I finally stopped. Even in such a chill environment Latifah was making me nervous. I thought that introducing her to Terrance could ease a little of the anxiety, but watching her watch me, was fucking me up.

As told by Terrance

Damn, Latifah was fine as fuck. I watched her approach Essence, so I had to introduce myself to her. I needed to get a piece of shorty.

"So, you got a man?" I spoke into her ear. The music was too loud to have a normal conversation, but I didn't mind. I could get close to her fine ass and inhale her scent. She smelled hella good, I could taste her.

"Nah." Her response was dry, but I ain't really give a fuck. The ladies love T, she would fall in line.

"You from around here?" I asked. Trying to keep the conversation going. She nodded her head yes.

"Why I never saw you before, you've been hiding from me?" She laughed. BINGO! I was breaking her down.

"Nah, nothing like that." She

continued to smile.

"So, I'm saying. What you doing after? We could link and get a bite to eat or something."

"Or we could go fuck." Her response sent me through the club's roof. I wasn't expecting that at all, but I was all for it.

"Oh, word?"

"Word." She stood up and took my hand, guiding me into the back of the club.

"Damn, Ma. You wild." The grin on my face increased as I watched her little ass in her catsuit switch. My dick rose at the sight. I licked my lips and followed closely behind her. Latifah stopped as we got to a door that read for employees only.

Latifah knocked three times, but no one answered. She took a key out of her purse and unlocked the door.

"What the fuck?" I said out loud.

"Don't worry, I got you." Latifah

turned around and looked at me before entering the dark room. Shit, fuck it. I walked in after her. She switched on the lights and the room was decked out like a bedroom.

"Yo, what's all this?" I was confused as hell. I almost forgot where we were until the music from the club vibrated through the walls.

"You wanna fuck, right?" She asked seductively. My mind screamed hell yeah, but I still had questions.

"Yeah, but…"

"No, buts. Come fuck me." Latifah cut me off. She walked towards the bed slowly peeling off her clothes. Her ass was as perfect out the catsuit as I imagined on the way back here. Without hesitation, I pulled my shirt over my head and unbuckled my belt to release my pants.

Latifah crawled into bed leaving her ass in the air. I licked my lips as I admired her arch. Latifah was a work of art. Her dark skin glowed. I ran my fingers across her smooth ass. Her back sunk in deeper and she let out a moan. I palmed her ass and she made her ass jump.

"Fuck me." She moaned out. Even with her on all fours in front of me, I couldn't believe this shit. I met her less than ten minutes ago and she was begging me to fuck her brains out. Well shit, if she asked for it Daddy T was gonna give it to her. I reached down to my pants at my ankle and pulled out a condom. I couldn't put it on fast enough before I was knee deep in her pussy.

"Ohhh." She called out. I gripped her waist thrusting myself inside her.

"Yeahhhh." I called back, enjoying every minute of it. I stepped out my pants without stopping. You can call that skill. I propped my right leg on the bed, so I could go deeper.

"I'm cumin' already." She stuttered. I

smiled at her response. Daddy T always delivered. You can call me the minute man, the only difference was, I made the bitches come in minutes. Jail probably had a lot to do with that. I spent too many nights jacking my shit. I built up enough stamina to sustain long rides.

I felt her walls closing in on my dick, followed by a gush of her juices. I pulled out of her and rolled her over on her stomach. I ripped the condom off and nutted all over her stomach.

"Dammmmn," I moaned, jacking the rest of my semen out of my dick. My eyes closed, as I continued to feel Latifah's hot pussy on my dick.

"You liked that? An unfamiliar voice spoke. My dick went limp as I felt cold metal on the back of my neck. I opened my eyes to see Latifah laying in bed, covered in my cum, with a huge grin on her face.

Fuck! I knew this shit was too good to

be true.

As told by Malcolm

"Hey, baby you ready to go?" All this dancing was making a nigga horny.

"Yup." Essence agreed.

I searched the room for Terrance.

"You see where Terrance went?"

Essence pointed over at the bar. "He was over there with Latifah." I followed Essence's finger, but Terrance was no longer there.

"Walk to the bathroom with me, I'm 'bout to see if I can call him." Hand in hand, we pushed ourselves through the crowd to the bathroom. Niggas was checking Essence out and bitches had their nose screwed up, when they realized she was with me. I smiled at them all.

Just when we reached the bathroom, I saw Terrance and the Latifah chick walking out a room across the hall.

"Yo, Terrance you good?" I asked.

"Yeah, I'm good." Terrance smiled. I glanced over at Latifah, who had a smile on her face too.

"Well, we bout to head out. You ready?"

"Um, nah. I'm gonna stay here and kick it with shorty for a little bit."

Essence and I looked at each other and then back at them too.

"Iight bet." I slapped Terrance up. He gave Essence a hug.

"Take care of my brother." Essence said to Latifah before hugging her.

"Oh, I will." Latifah replied with a grin. I nodded my head at Terrance and grabbed Essence's hand. It was cold as hell outside, I pulled Essence close to me as we walked to the car.

"Latifah good people?" I asked Essence when we were situated in the car.

"She cool. Why you ask?"

"Oh nah, its nothing." I shook my

head, but it was something about her that didn't sit well with me. You can tell a lot about a person through their eyes, and her shits were dark. I felt it as soon as she glared into mine when we shook hands.

CHAPTER 3

As told by Malcolm

I met Terrance down at Jones Place. We were finalizing the plans for the new and improved building. The apartment had the ability to house over a hundred families, but only a few were occupied. This was a good thing because it would cost us more money to relocate these families into other places. For now, all we had to do was renovate the abandoned ones first and move the families into a remodeled apartment while the rest got done. Our time frame was four months; by April the weather would be much better and we could start to do the outside. The task would be something, but it was going to get done.

"Hello fellas." Walt greeted us looking like the Uncle Tom nigga he was. I nodded at him and Terrance didn't speak. Walt laughed nervously.

"I don't want any beef. I was just stopping by to say congratulations and good luck."

Terrance was grilling a hole in Walt's face, so much I could see steam. I watched Terrance clench his teeth as if he was stopping himself from acting on his thoughts.

"Thanks man." I answered. I wanted Walt out of our presence. Ain't no telling what Terrance was ready to do. Walt just smiled and left.

"What was that for?" I asked rhetorically.

"I don't know, but I just want to crack that nigga." Terrance roared, hitting his fist to his palm.

I attempted to calm Terrance down, "he ain't even worth it bro. We got what we wanted." I smiled lifting my hands up.

"You right, but that nigga need to be the one to do so."

I laughed at Terrance, shaking my head. It wasn't funny because I know he meant every word. It was easier for me to brush off Walt's antics, but not so easy for Terrance.

Walt and Terrance had history. We were all from Jones Place although we were never cool with Walt. He ended up getting locked up with Terrance a few years after Terrance's bid started and they linked up. Terrance didn't fuck with the other inmates. He stayed to himself. His mission was not to make friends, but to do his time and bounce. Walt came along, and swayed his mind a little bit. Walt told him it would be better if they stuck together since they were from the same hood. Terrance had Walt's back a hundred grand because that's just who Terrance is. He held his own, so he didn't need much assistance, but it was nice to know if he needed Walt, he was there.

The judge ended up granting Walt an early release, so instead of doing a full ten, he only did seven. Terrance was happy for Walt, even though he had three years left on the inside himself.

Walt swore to hold Terrance down once he got out, but he ain't keep his promises. No visits, calls or money on his books. He did a whole 180, started dressing differently, acting differently and everything. He even acted as if he didn't know Terrance. Terrance brushed it off, but it still left a bad taste in his mouth and it should.

We didn't even know dude had anything to do with Jones Place when we first inquired, but come to find out, Walt's uncle signed the deed over to him when he got released, as a welcome home gift. He gave us the run around for months, but once he caught wind it was us bidding on the apartments, he gave in. Terrance's hardcore demeanor was enough to scare anybody off, but Walt knew he had fucked up and didn't want to take any chances. Shit, if we knew it was his bitch ass playing all these games, we could've had this shit on lock a long time ago. Walt could pretend like he ain't know Terrance, but faking gets you nowhere. He began requesting to meet with me instead of Terrance but fuck that. I made it my business that Terrance was available to go.

"Wassup with shorty Essence introduced you to Friday night?" I attempted to change the subject and it worked. I honestly couldn't keep the whole Latifah thing off my mind. It was more to her and I hoped Terrance wasn't blinded by her.

Terrance rubbed his hands together and licked his lips like he was LL Cool J.

"She cool." Terrance pretended to be humble.

I laughed, "Cool? Nigga you are smiling like you fucked her." I clowned.

Terrance just smiled.

"Damn, my nigga already?" I knew Terrance fucked that night, it was all over his face when they came out the room.

He didn't say anything, he just started walking ahead.

"Damn, it's like that." Terrance never really bragged about the bitches he was fucking, but that was a dead giveaway.

Even though it appeared Terrance had left the conversation, I followed him. "You feeling her?"

"Damn, nigga what's with all the questions?" I could sense his annoyance.

"Nothin' bro, I'd just like to see you settle down some day." I tried not to lead him on to my suspicions of her.

"Shit. I'd like to see it too." Terrance admitted. "Ma won't leave me alone about it. She buggin' 'bout the grandkids though." We shared a laugh.

"You better make Ms. Sheila some grandbabies." I rubbed it in a little more. As long as he ain't make Latifah his baby mama, we were good.

Ring! Ring! Terrance phone started to ring.

"I'm on my way," He answered and hung up,

"Hey, look. I gotta get ghost," Terrance pleaded, "I gotta...handle something right quick."

"Iight, bet."

As told by Terrance

I'm glad my phone rang when it did. I was hoping Malcolm would stop asking me questions about Latifah. It wasn't in my DNA to be keeping shit from him, but until I found a way to shake her, I had no choice.

I spent 15 years in prison and a nigga never tried me. I'm from one of the toughest hoods in Chicago. Niggas knew better than to fuck with me. By the tender age of 13 I was running shit, and it ain't stop when I got locked up at 19. My name held weight. But, this bitch in a skin tight catsuit got me. Whoever said pussy didn't hold the power, was a got damn lie.

I cruised through the streets on my way to Stone, replaying our encounter the other night.

"Move and I'll shoot your fucking brains out," the unfamiliar voice retorted. With the cold steel up against my neck, I didn't dare move. I didn't know who it was behind this gun. The nigga could've been calling my bluff, but I wasn't taking any chances.

"Latifah, tell this punk bitch what he's won." The man ordered her.

"Damn nigga can I clean myself up first?"

She snapped back and rolled her eyes.

"Look Terrance. That crazy mutherfucker holding the gun back there is looking for fresh meat."

"Fresh meat? Look shorty, enough with the small talk. What the fuck is going on?" I growled. I was standing naked with a gun to my head and this bitch was speaking in code.

"Aye, calm down." The man laughed.

"Fuck you!" I spat, causing him to laugh louder.

"I gotta give it to you Latifah, you picked a good one this time."

Latifah rolled her eyes, and pulled her outfit back on.

"Look we got a huge opportunity for you." I grilled her without speaking.

"I've been watching you all night and I think you'll be beneficial for our team."

"Latifah, cut all this kumbaya shit and tell the nigga wassup."

"Would you shut the fuck up and let me do me." Latifah rolled her eyes again. I was with *him tho, my tolerance was low as fuck with this conversation.*

"Meet us here on Monday. Just come around the back."

"And if I don't?" They must think I'm stupid. I don't know what bullshit they got going on, but I don't want no parts of it. They dumb as fuck if they think I was gonna meet them here.

"You will, we know where to find you." Ol' boy answered before Latifah did.

"Please Terrance, we need you." She pleaded.

"Please Terrance, we need you," he mocked her. "Get dressed!" He smashed the barrel into my neck before lowering the gun. I turned quick to knock this nigga out, but I was face to face, staring down the barrel of a silver desert eagle 50 caliber.

"Get dressed." He spoke through clenched teeth. I made sure not to take my eyes off him. I wanted to remember his face. I smirked as I pictured myself, blowing his pretty little green eyes out their fucking sockets.

"I'm so glad you can join us." Latifah answered the back door. I was here to mirk her and her bitch ass accomplice, but my dick missed the memo. One look at her made my dick hard.

"Yeah, yeah. What's this all about?" I asked, trying not to focus my attention on her.

"Relax, don't be so uptight." She stepped closer to me and massaged my shoulders. She smelled just as good as she did the other night.

Latifah whispered in my ear, "You happy to see me?" She referenced towards my hard-on, reaching down to touch it, her hand swept across my dick before reaching for my gun.

She pulled the gun off my waist and smiled, "You won't be needing this." I gritted my teeth. This bitch was smart. She placed my gun in her purse and walked away. I followed her, once again.

"Hey, pal. Nice to see you again." Dude from the other night, stood up and extended his hand. I looked down at his hand and back at him. He laughed.

"You are a tough son of a bitch. I like you." He sat back down and took a drink from his cup. "Have a seat." He pointed for me to sit down.

"I'll stand," I answered.

"Be my guest," he responded, laughing again. Latifah sat down next to him.

"Terrance, Latifah here thinks you may be a good fit for our establishment."

"Yo, quit the bullshit. Stop beating around the bush and tell me what's good."

"We need you to manage some girls for us." Latifah blurted out.

"Manage some girls?" I laughed. "What the fuck I look like? Man, I'm out of here." I turned to walk around.

"I don't think you want to do that." Latifah stopped me.

"Fuck ya'll." I started walking towards the door, "give me back my piece."

Latifah stood up without hesitation. She reached into her purse and pulled out my gun to hand it to me. When she reached in, a picture fell out of her purse.

"Oops," she said, bending down to pick up the paper. Handing me both the gun and the paper, I began to hand the paper back to her, before I realized it was a picture of Ma Dukes on it.

Ol' boy sat on the couch wearing a sinister's smile.

"How the fuck you get this?" I asked. My body filled with rage.

"None of that matters, just know we got it. So, you have no choice, but to join our team or Ms. Sheila here is gone." I shook my head in disbelief.

"What I gotta do?" I asked.

"Now you're talking." Dude, sat up and rubbed his hands together. He went on to explain to me the process. They would trick girls into thinking they got a modeling gig and auction them off at events. Crazy thing about it was that they did it out in the open, each night Stone was open, there was opportunity for a trade to be going on. These men paid big bucks for these women. They needed me to help recruit more girls. Latifah said it was my good looks and charm that would attract the girls. At the same time, my size was enough to intimidate the girls. The shit was twisted. They were on some real life human trafficking type shit. My stomach turned at the thought of it all.

I had no other option but to oblige…for now. Latifah walked me to the door.

"Hey, Terrance," she whispered before turning back to look at ol' boy on the couch.

"What?"

"Don't tell anyone about this, please. Especially Malcolm or Essence."

CHAPTER 4

As told by Essence

I was adjusting to Chicago well. I didn't think the transition would be so easy, but it wasn't bad at all. Although, I was used to calling all the shots, *Jackson & Jackson* had been treating me well. Vincent wanted to start off the new year with a bonus issue presenting *Jo Nova*. I was honored when he announced the project. All I've been doing was giving input for *Jackson & Jackson*, and now I was getting a little more leeway. The amount of work I put into this was tremendous, but it was worth it. The final touches were the photoshoot Latifah scheduled today.

I walked into the studio, admiring all the tall, slender figures in the room. They were of all shades of color. Latifah really outdid herself. There was no doubt that she was really official with everything she did.

"See something you like?" Latifah came up behind me, startling me.

"Girl, you scared me." I jumped, placing my hand over my heart. Latifah touched my hand and brought it back to my side.

"Don't be scared." Latifah stared at me for a while.

"These girls are beautiful, where did you find them?" I asked attempting to change the subject and take some of the anxious weight off my shoulders.

"I wouldn't be your go to girl if I told all my secrets." Latifah winked and walked away.

I watched Latifah head over to the girls. She walked over to the girls and directed them to where they needed to be. Without question, they followed her commands. She was like a puppet master using her deep brown eyes as the strings.

"Sorry, I'm so sorry. Excuse me." One of the models apologized after bumping in to me.

"It's okay love." I was actually glad she broke me out of my trance.

"Lydia, is everything okay?" Latifah walked up behind us.

"Yes, yes, Miss Washington." Fear plastered all over her face as she hurried off.

"Essence, your work is extraordinary." Vincent smiled as he flipped through the rough draft. It was like déjà vu, almost a year ago, I was in this same office, waiting for him to assign my fate, less stressful of course. I was already in, but I still wanted it to be superb.

"I think we are ready for the New Year's Eve launch. What do you think?"

"I'm from Inglewood, we stay ready." I humored, but it was nothing but the truth behind it. Vincent joined me in laughter.

"What's so funny?" Latifah asked ceasing our laughs.

"Oh nothing." Vincent shooed her off.

"Essence, when you guys are done with your little comedy showdown, I need to talk to you."

Vincent waved Latifah off. "Look, Essence. Latifah has all the details for the launch. Make sure you bring Malcolm."

"Sure will." I left Vincent's office on the highest horse. Latifah stood up when I approached her desk.

"Sooo, how did your meeting with Vincent go?"

"He loved it!"

Latifah started clapping, "Aye, I told

you!" Latifah exclaimed pulling me in for a hug. Her perfume was heavenly and her touch was just as I had imagined.

I pulled back from her, "yes, yes you did. Vincent said you had details for the launch."

"Oh yes." Latifah fumbled through papers on her desk and pulled out an envelope and handed it to me. She brushed her hands against mine as I took the envelope. I stared at her bright red nail polish because I couldn't dare look her in the eyes.

"Are you going to invite Terrance?" I asked. Latifah hadn't mentioned much about Terrance, but I knew from Malcolm they were still kicking it.

"Yup, he will be there.

"Malcolm?" Latifah shot me a smile.

"Of course." I smiled back before heading back to my office.

My pussy was throbbing and in need of a release. I am team Strictly Dickly, but

Latifah was reaching a part of me that I didn't know existed.

Later that night, my mind was still fixated on Latifah. As Malcolm kissed me, I pretended it was Latifah who was kissing me. When he touched me, his muscular hands were replaced with Latifah's soft hands painted in her infamous bright red nail polish. Malcolm going down on me was enough to release what I had built up all day. As he licked his lips and kissed me. It was Latifah's smooth round face that I saw instead of his.

As told by Malcolm

"Baby, you okay?" I asked Essence. She was acting a little strange since she got home from work. Even as we made love her body wasn't as receptive as it usually is. It was clear her mind was somewhere else, but I continued my duty as her pleaser. I figured she had a lot of things on her mind. Today was approval day with Vincent and she hadn't mentioned one thing about it.

"Yes, I'm fine."

"Did your meeting with Vincent go well?" I asked.

"It went great. *Jackson & Jackson* is hosting a New Year's Eve party at Stone to reveal this issue."

I stood up on my forearm, "That's great, baby. You don't sound happy about it.

Essence turned to me, displaying a forced smile, "I am happy. Just a little stressed."

"Come here," I pulled Essence close to me.

We laid in silence with Essence's head on my chest until she fell asleep. It took me a little longer to fall asleep. I rattled my brain, trying to figure out Essence's new vibe. She moved to Chicago for this opportunity and now that it presented itself, she didn't seem pleased. I know it was bothering her more than she led on, but I'll give her time to reveal.

The next morning, I got up early to head to the office. I left breakfast for Essence on the bedside table and packed her a lunch on the counter. I sealed it with a love note. It was my duty to make sure Essence was straight, so anything I could do to help, I would.

"Aye, you here early." I spoke to Terrance. Terrance was not an early bird by any means. I was surprised to see him.

"You know, I'm turning over a new leaf." Terrance popped his collar, making me laugh.

"Yeah right, you up to something." I suggested.

He laughed, "Just crunching some numbers. Latifah asked me to accompany her to some party on New Year's Eve, so we going shopping later."

"She got you tricking bro?"

"Tricking?" Terrance's face got serious, "hell nah, I don't trick."

I chuckled, "Damn man, relax. It was just a joke. The all-black joint?" I inquired.

"Yeah, yeah, that," Terrance nodded his head.

"Essence told me a little about it last night, I gotta find some shit to wear too. It's my baby's debut, you know a nigga gotta look sharp." I ran my pinky fingers across my eyebrows.

"Nigga, you ain't sharp."

"Yeah, don't be hating." Terrance's phone rang.

"Yo. Yeah, I know. Noon. I got you. I said I got you. Iight. Iight." Terrance hung up the phone shaking his head.

"Latifah?"

"How'd you know?" He asked.

"Your face said it all, women don't play when it comes to looking fly at an event. She bout to have you in some high waters and loafers."

"Hell nah." Terrance looked back at his laptop.

"You might got a good one there." I stirred the pot, knowing it was complete bullshit. Latifah was not the one for him.

"You already know, you gotta good one." Terrance changed the focus to me.

I just shook my head. Terrance was right. Essence was a good one.

Terrance headed out the office around 11:45 to go meet up with Latifah.

All the other properties associated with Hill Homes were straight and since Jones Place was the priority at the time, I decided to go check in. The renovations of Jones Place were going just as we wanted them to go. The contractors were about their bread, they fulfilled every task, whether big or small. They were ahead of schedule and I was pleased. It was even better than I imagined it to be. My favorite part was the community center we were building on the ground floor. I feel as if it is important for the kids to have a safe place to go and vibe with other kids. They wouldn't have to travel far and the amenities I was setting up were going to be rewarding for them.

I had enough micromanaging what was going on at Jones Place and decided to head home.

When I got to the car I took my phone out to call Essence, but I already had a text from her saying she was just leaving work and was headed home.

Essence was so considerate. She was always thinking of others before herself. Especially when it came to me. She understood balance and compromise. She understood that we were a team, so everything she did affected the both of us; good, bad or indifferent. She also understood that I was aware of the same thing. I believe we bonded so well because we were alike in many ways. A lot of qualities I possessed, she possessed so it was easy understanding each other.

I smiled thinking about Essence. I know I wanted her to be my wife, it was just the matter of me picking out her ring. I wanted to ask Joanne & Unique for their blessings, first. I was scared to take this step, but nonetheless, ready.

This black Chrysler been behind me for a minute, I thought to myself. I feel like this car has been behind me since I left Jones Place. I made a right turn and sure enough the black Chrysler turned too. When I made a left so did they.

"What the fuck?" I spoke out loud. I dialed Terrance's number and it rang until it reached the voicemail. I dialed again and the same thing.

"Yo, T. Man, it's a black Chrysler license plate number XXX 0000, following behind me. I'm tryna lose them, but hit me when you done. And check this shit out for me."

"Fuck!" I screamed as the car continued to follow me. I decided to pull over and see what their move would be. To my surprise the car pulled beside me and slowed down. I reached in my glove compartment to grab my Smith and Wesson. The tint was too dark for me to peep who was in the car. For a split second the car stopped and rolled the back window down just a little and I aimed my Smith & Wesson up. It was cocked and ready to go. A hand with a black leather glove reached out the window and flicked a cigar out the window. The car rolled off leaving me there huffing and puffing. I ain't want to kill anybody, but I was ready if need be.

I watched the car speed off and turn left off the Ave. I got out the car and scoped my surroundings. I picked up the cigar and read the wrapper. There was a black wrapper with HLC written in gold letters.

"HLC? HLC? The fuck is HLC?" I asked myself out loud. I've never heard of any cigars with this name, it must've been specially made. Whoever dropped it, was sending me a message. It wasn't even lit.

I was paranoid the entire ride home. I took the scenic route to make sure I was no longer being followed. When I knew the coast was clear, I turned into the driveway and pulled into the garage.

"Hey, handsome." Essence greeted me at the door. She was in a better mood then she had been in a while.

"Hey." My response was dry, but I was trying to piece my mind together with what just went down.

"Eww." Essence's face was screwed up at me.

"Sorry, baby. I just…I have a lot on my mind. I apologize."

"It's cool." Essence wasn't believable, but I couldn't entertain that at this moment. I needed to speak with Terrance.

"Call Terrance please."

Essence's face filled with concern, "Everything okay?" she asked.

"Yeah, yeah. My phone is dead." I didn't mean to lie to Essence, but it was better than getting her worked up about what just happened. Essence dialed Terrance's number and it went straight to voicemail.

Where the fuck is this nigga? I thought to myself. He couldn't still be out shopping with Latifah. I needed him ASAP. My mind wouldn't rest until I got the information I needed.

As told by Terrance

I was in desperate need of a way out of this deal with Latifah. Lying to my right hand was not sitting well with me. I sat at the dinner table waiting for one of the girls to show up.

I'M OUT LATIFAH! I texted her.

It took a while before she texted back and when she did, it was another picture of Mama. Fuck! This bitch ain't playing fair.

"Hey, I'm Tara." A voice spoke to me.

"Hey, I'm uh Larry." I stood up and shook her hand. As I sat across from Tara, I wanted to tell her to run away. Her innocence showed as she flipped through her pictures on her phone telling me all her dreams. I felt like scum as I sat there and fed her false hope, knowing damn well I had no plans to take her modeling career to the next level.

My response was rehearsed, but she was so young and naïve she couldn't read through it. Tara wasn't the only girl I met that day. It was Tisha, Janay, Sara, Sam, Kisha, I could go on. All beautiful young women, with no idea what they were getting themselves into.

It was late by the time I was done with

them fake ass auditions. I felt my phone buzz, it was Malcolm calling me. I turned my phone off. I wasn't in the mood to lie to him, I had to get home and formulate a plan.

CHAPTER 5

As told by Malcolm

I tossed and turned all night. I still haven't heard from Terrance and I was getting a little worried. He was usually good with returning calls. Especially messages like that; he would have called back by now.

"Baby, you were up all night." Essence rolled over and kissed my shoulder blade.

"I apologize for keeping you up. I'm worried about Terrance." It was part of the truth, but enough to keep her from inquiring more information. I didn't even have any to give her if she did ask.

Essence sat up in bed. "What happened to him? Is he okay? Malcolm what's going on?" Essence fired off question after question before I could respond.

"I haven't heard from him since he left Jones Place earlier. He was in a rush and it was the same behavior I've seen from him for the last couple weeks."

"What do you think is going on with him?"

I let out a sigh, "I'm not sure baby, but I will find out." I was ready to find out about a couple of things and I needed Terrance's help to do that. It was too bad I had to try and figure him out too.

I grabbed my phone off the charger to dial Terrance again, this time he answered.

"Yo, its 6:30 in the morning, bro. You good?" I was happy to hear Terrance's voice, but upset that he didn't call back when he noticed I left a voicemail.

"My nigga, I've been calling you all

fucking night. Where you been at?"

"Mal, chill. I told you I had a few things to handle. Wassup though?" Terrance changed the subject quickly.

I looked at Essence who was hanging on to every word we spoke. "Check your voicemail. I'll meet you at Hill Homes in an hour."

"Bet."

"Bet." When I hung up, Essence was staring me down as if she wanted to hurt me.

"Baby, its boring work stuff." I tried to belittle the situation. Essence rolled her eyes giving me another look of death. I kissed her cheek and headed to the bathroom to get ready. I hope Terrance didn't call back when I was in the shower. All I needed was her answering my phone and Terrance telling all what he found out, without realizing it was Essence he was talking to.

When I was done in the shower

Essence was still in bed. She was usually out of bed and halfway dressed for work by now.

"No work?" I asked as I got dressed.

"Nope. Not today. Just gonna hang out around here all day and do absolutely nothing." Essence forced a smile. I could tell it was still bothering her, but once I get everything in line, I will fill her in. This has been a crazy year for Essence and I was trying to be mindful of that.

"Okay, baby. I love you."

"I love you too."

I was paranoid as hell going into the office. After being followed last night, I had to keep my radar open. Shit, I ain't have beef in Chicago. I don't know what the fuck was going on. Terrance's car was already parked and he was outside waiting for me.

"What took you so long nigga?" Terrance asked.

"You got something for me?" I wasn't

feeling Terrance's attitude, but I'd address that later. Right now, I needed to see what he knew.

"Let's go inside." Terrance walked ahead of me and I followed close behind him. I looked back and forth for anything suspicious.

"So wassup?" I asked as soon as we were inside.

"I called my people up soon as I listened to the voicemail. Look, my bad I didn't pick up. I was…busy." Terrance pleaded his case.

"Yeah. You told me that. Wassup with that Chrysler?" We could get into his weird behavior another time. I wanted to know who was following me.

"My people ran the plate and the name came back to some old bitch named Sara Smith."

"Smith. Smith. Oh shit. Shanell's last name is Smith." A lightbulb went off in my head. How the fuck did Shanell's people find me and what did they want? Gennie was the one that offed the bitch. "Nah bro. It ain't even that. she ain't got no ties to Shanell."

"How you know?"

"My boys already pressed her. She said her car was stolen." *Damn.* I thought to myself. I'm glad it wasn't Shanell's people, but who else could it be?

"Do you know who stole it?"

"Nah, that's the fucked up part about it. They don't know who stole it. Whoever it was, was smooth. You know my young boys find out anything. Look how quick they got that bitch address." Terrance started pacing.

I put my head in my hands.

"Did you see a face?" Terrance asked.

"If I saw a face, you think we would be here tryna…" I stopped as I remembered I didn't mention the cigar to him.

Terrance could see my face change.

"What you thinking?"

"Yo, I forgot to tell you these niggas pulled up beside me and dropped a cigar out the window.

"And?" This stopped Terrance from pacing.

"And the wrapper had HLC on it, in gold letters."

"HLC?" Terrance asked,

"HLC!" I repeated and we both looked at each other, as we thought the same thing.

"Howard Luigi Crespo."

"Hell nah, man." Terrance shook his head.

That son of a bitch deserved to die. Gennie's evil voice replayed in my head. Gennie left for Germany, Terrance made sure to follow up on that. Howard and his goons was dead. So, who the fuck could this be?

"What the fuck! Everybody is dead.Howard and his bitch ass boys is dead. Gennie in Germany. Shanell is gone. I'm all out of suspects." Terrance was pacing again.

"Me too. Me too." I agreed. Just as I went through all the potentials, so did Terrance. There was not one person on our radar.

Ring. Ring. Terrance's phone rang.

"Yo, I can't right now I'm a little busy." Terrance turned away from me, "I said I'm busy…damn man, okay."

Terrance walked back over to me.

"Who was that?" I asked. With all this shit going on, Terrance and his suspicious activities got me on edge.

"Ain't shit. Look, imma hit up my young boys and see if they heard anything. I'll holla at you inna minute." I couldn't even contest to it, even if I wanted to. It just wasn't in me. My mind immediately went to Essence. She had no idea how much danger she could be in, but I wanted to keep it that way.

Terrance and I were going to get to the bottom of this and Essence didn't need to know.

As told by Terrance

My heart dropped to the pit of my stomach, when I finally listened to Malcolm's voicemail. If there wasn't a better reason for me to shake off Latifah and her little green-eyed sidekick, there was now.

I've had Malcolm's back since we were little boys in Jones Place. He held me down when I was away and got me right when I was released. I owed it to him. In no time, my young boys were on it, but it left us at a dead end. It had Latifah's name all over it. Malcolm ain't have no beef, he was a stand-up guy. She already threatened to get close to Ma Dukes, so I'm sure this bitch would do anything to make sure I didn't back out.

Essence knew some fucked up people

yo. I can't imagine why a woman like her, with so much shit going for herself kept associating herself with these shiesty bitches. Latifah was a good actress though. Her eyes were enough to drive a nigga wild, but the bitch was a savage. Cold-hearted and cold-blooded.

It wasn't until Malcolm remembered that cigar he found that my mind changed. Crespo! That grease ball was six feet under and still causing problems. My plate was getting full and I wasn't up to eating.

Ring. Ring. My phone rang breaking Malcolm and I out of our debriefing.

"Meet me at Stone." Latifah commanded.

"Yo, I can't right now I'm a little busy." I turned my back to Malcolm. I could feel him looking at me, but I couldn't face looking him in the eye.

"See you in 10." She responded. Ignoring the fact that I was in the middle of something.

"I said I'm busy." I yelled to her.

"I wonder what Sheila's up to today?" Latifah laughed. My jaw shut tight, as the veins on the side of my face pierced through my skin, exaggerating my anger.

"Damn man, okay." I hung up without giving her a chance to respond. Just as I thought, Malcolm was watching me. I figured it would ease his mind if I told him my boys was on it. The look on his face confirmed that he didn't believe me.

As told by Essence

I wasn't sure what was up with Malcolm, but sooner than later, I was going to find out.

"Hey beautiful." Latifah answered on the first ring.

Trying to keep my composure, I replied, "Good morning. I have a question."

"You can ask me anything." I could

hear Latifah smiling through the phone.

"Well, Mal has been trying to get in touch with Terrance all night. You talked to Terrance?"

"Uh, no. No, why'd you ask?" Latifah stuttered.

"Something fishy, is going on with them two." I admitted.

"Fishy?"

"Yeah. Malcolm rushed out of here this morning when he finally got a hold of him."

"Maybe, its work?" Latifah suggested. She was right, Malcolm made it his business to not lie to me.

"You're right. How have you two been anyway?" I was curious to know.

"We're iight."

"Iight, that's it?" Latifah never wanted to talk about Terrance. I wasn't trying to get all in her business, but the curiosity was killing me.

"Yup, but it's cool. He isn't the one I

want anyway."

My heart pounded through my chest at her comment. I know the "one" she was referring to was me.

"Latifah, I gotta go." I rushed off the phone.

"Goodbye beautiful." Latifah purred before hanging up.

My concern for Malcolm and Terrance was quickly replaced with the thought of Latifah and I. My thoughts were completely wrong, but they were out of my control. If Malcolm knew I was crushing on someone else, he would be devastated. Nonetheless it was a woman and she was currently dating Terrance.

CHAPTER 6

As told by Essence

I watched Malcolm as he stood in the mirror watching me. We were both looking at each other, but it was as if we were looking through each other. The eye contact we shared screamed secrets. He is holding back from me and I am holding back from him.

Even with the guilt I felt, day in and day out, it wasn't enough for me to stop fantasizing. It wasn't enough for me to be truthful with Malcolm and let him know what's been on my mind. I wasn't even brave enough to tell Latifah how I felt.

Regardless of the passes she makes at me I was trying my hardest to not show interest.

Malcolm had a sincere look of worry on his face. It has been two weeks since he ran off to talk to Terrance and he hasn't brought up the conversation. For some reason, I think it can affect me. He tried to brush it off as work-related, but the way he looked at me was concerning. He hugged me just a little bit tighter and kissed me a little bit longer. He was calling and texting me more frequently. All cute simple gestures, but it was more than usual.

"Baby is everything okay?" I broke our silent stare.

Malcolm turned around to face me. "Yes. Everything is fine."

"Malcolm you're lying to me." Tears welled up in my eyes. It hurt to have him look me in my eyes and lie.

"Essence everything is fine. You have

no worries. I'll handle it. When it's time for you to know, I'll tell you." His voice was stern, but not the usual stern voice that turned me on.

"Malcolm, that's bullshit." I exclaimed, "pure bullshit and you know it!" I was beyond pissed. Yes, it's cool that Malcolm was always trying to protect me. I totally trust that he would handle whatever "it" is, but I didn't like that he left me out of the loop.

"Essence…" He started.

"No, Malcolm. I'm not a kid. You can't protect me from everything."

"I can and I will. As long as you're my lady; as long as I'm on this earth." Malcolm's words were passionate. I felt every word he said to be true.

Malcolm had the final word. He kissed my forehead and walked out. Tears rolled off my cheeks. How could I not love him? How can I not be happy that I have a man like him protecting me? How can I still yearn for Latifah's touch?

It was hard for me to focus at work. The launch party was just days away. I had so much work to do. It was important that I stayed on top of things. I needed everything to be perfect! This launch would be the best way to start off the new year. 2016 has been a crazy year and I was ready to forget about it.

Knock! Knock! Of course, to make matters more complicated, Latifah was at my door.

"Hey beautiful. A few of us are going out after work, you wanna join?"

"No, no. I have a lot to do. Maybe next time." I turned down the invitation.

"Come on Essence! You've been walking around here so uptight lately. The magazine is fine. The launch will be fine! Come out with us. Pleeassseeee!" Latifah begged. She didn't have to do much to convince me. I already wanted to be where she was I didn't turn down the invite because of work, I turned it down because I didn't know how much longer I could be around her today.

"Okay. Okay. Let me just ask Malcolm."

"Ask Malcolm?" Latifah seemed annoyed. "You don't see me calling to ask Terrance." Latifah laughed and left the office. A slight hint of jealousy came over me as she reminded me of her and Terrance's relationship. Part of me thinks she did it just because. I know she wasn't in to him like she was in to me.

I sent Malcolm a quick text letting him know my plans. He told me to be safe and have fun, but not too much fun. I laughed at his humor. It was nice to know he was much less tense since our conversation this morning. I let out a breath in attempt to prepare myself for later.

Latifah, Vincent and two other co-workers went out to a bar down the street from *Jackson & Jackson*. We laughed, danced, and had plenty of drinks.

"Essence, what made you move to Chicago?" Maria, one of my co-workers, asked.

I haven't really talked about personal business with anyone at work. I kept our relationship professional because that was what's best. Even with a few drinks in me, I still honored that.

"It was just time for a change. The city was good to me, but I needed something different.

"Like Malcolm?" Vincent blurted out and we all laughed. Everyone knew about Malcolm. He made himself known from day one. If they knew anything about me it was the love I had for Malcolm. I peeped over at Latifah who had stopped laughing and sipped her drink. She saw me looking at her and raised her eyebrow.

"Look guys. I had a ball tonight, but I think it's time for me to call it a night."

"Aww…really?" Frank, another co-worker whined.

"Yes. I can't hang as long as ya'll. Plus, I gotta get home to my man."

"Yes, you do that honey." Frank snapped his fingers three times.

Latifah got up as I did and gathered her things, "I'm going to take it in too guys."

"Aww…not you too!" Frank whined again.

Maria slurred, "Let them go. Party poopers," Maria stuck out her tongue and we all laughed. We gave out hugs and walked out the bar hand in hand. Latifah and I laughed at nothing.

When we got to my car Latifah gave me a hug good night. Her hands gripped my ass firmly, catching me by surprise. Although I was surprised, I was immediately in heat. I've been waiting for this moment.

Latifah looked me into my eyes before we met each other halfway and kissed. Her lips were warm, just as I imagined. Her soft hands massaged my ass, just as I imagined. We let out small moans as our tongues whirled around each other's mouths. My hands began to explore Latifah's thin frame.

Warm tears fell from my eyes as I passionately kissed this woman as if she was the love of my life. This was not a daydream in my daily collection. It was really happening and it was perfect, just as I imagined it to be.

We shared each other's chemistry for a little while longer until Latifah finally broke our seal.

"Damn, beautiful I've been waiting for that." Latifah smiled at me and walked away.

"Me too!" I spoke under my breath.

As told by Terrance

I can't believe what the fuck I just saw, Essence and Latifah making out. Hell nah, my eyes must've been deceiving me. Ain't no way in hell Essence on some shit like that. Damn, man. How the fuck am I going to bring some shit up like that to Malcolm.

I waited until Essence drove off to approach Latifah who was also watching Essence pull off. I knocked on her car window causing her to jump.

"What the fuck? You scared the shit out of me." Latifah spat rolling her window down.

"What was that about?"

She looked at me with a face of confusion, "What was what about?"

"Don't play fucking stupid Latifah."

"Terrance, look…" She began.

I put my hands up to silence her, "I'm going to tell you once and never a fucking 'gain. You leave Essence alone or

I will kill you."

Latifah smiled.

"I'm not fucking playing with you. She's been through enough shit, yo."

"You don't understand, Terrance." She pleaded.

"I understand you's a shiesty bitch, that like to seduce people into doing fucked up shit. Leave her out of it."

"I would never do that to her." Latifah's face softened up, it wasn't an expression that I was used to seeing. Was she really feeling Essence?

"I don't know that, but what I do know is that you better back the fuck off." I grilled her to make my point, before walking away.

I couldn't believe Essence. Not my sis, I know she wouldn't do this to my mans. This had Latifah's name all over it. She waited until she was tipsy and vulnerable to try one on her, just like she did me. I can hold my own though, but not

Essence. Essence wasn't about to get involved with any of this shit. I bet my life on that.

As told by Essence

Oh my God. Oh my God. Oh my God. I can't believe that just happened. I just tongued down a chick in the middle of the sidewalk. It had to be the Long Islands. It wasn't forced, it was just right.

Ring! Ring! Malcolm was calling. Fuck! Malcolm. What was I going to tell him? I didn't answer his call, I was too nervous to hear his voice. He sent me a text.

HEY BABY. JUST CHECKIN IN WIT U. U MUST B HAVIN FUN. C U WHEN U GET HOME.

I was having fun alright, fun twirling my tongue down Latifah's throat. It's like she put a spell on me, like every time she looked at me with those dreamy eyes and half smirk, she was reeling me in.

I sat in the driveway for a while, trying

to gather my thoughts before I went in the house. Malcolm would be up waiting for me to give him a rundown of my night. It was my first night going out without him.

"Heyyy." Malcolm greeted me as soon as I walked in.

"Hey baby." I smiled, trying to hide my guilt.

I must've failed because it led him to ask, "You okay? You don't look like you had a good time."

"I'm well, baby," I leaned in to kiss him and again Latifah's feminine face interchanged with his strong cheekbones. I jumped back.

"Essence, is there something you need to tell me?" Malcolm searched my face for answers, but I had none to give. I know what I should be saying. I just wasn't equipped to confess right now. Malcolm didn't wait for an answer. He picked me up over his shoulder and carried me upstairs. I let out a sigh.

Malcolm was the man of my dreams. I loved him like no other. I'd never do anything to intentionally hurt him, but when the urge keeps knocking, how do you not answer?

As told by Malcolm

I could tell Essence was still a little shook up from our little argument this morning. I hated that it had to be this way, but it was best. Terrance still didn't have any information regarding the Crespo situation. It just wasn't a good time to tell her. Once our ducks were aligned, she would be updated. Until then, I will guard her, like my life depended on it.

CHAPTER 7

As told by Terrance

Latifah requested I meet her down at Stone, before the party started. Tonight was my first official secret auction.

"Now look, you don't have to do much. There's only four girls for you to keep an eye on. All four will be in our VIP section tonight." Latifah pulled out pictures of the girls. Two of them were the shorties I met the other day. The excitement in their eyes had faded. Their beauty was still evident, but you could tell by the pictures that their last couple weeks of life have been rough.

My stomach started to get upset at the thought. I've done some fucked up shit in the past, but selling pussy was not ever on my to-do list. It's not even like these poor girls wanted to be escorts. They were forced to be.

"You listening?" Latifah asked, rolling her eyes with her hand on her hips.

"Yeah, man I hear you." I was ready to get this shit done with.

"You got a smart-ass mouth, you know that?" Latifah smiled.

I wasn't in a smiling mood. I still hadn't forgot about the other night. I wanted to bash her fucking head in. I already been holding on to the anger I had about the pictures of Ma Dukes she was threatening me with.

"Latifah, on the real. Why you do shit like this?"

Latifah looked at me and sighed. I searched her face for a response, but didn't get one.

"Ready?" She perked up suddenly and downed the last bit of drink she had left. All I could do was shake my head.

"Heyy pal!" My body tensed at his voice. Latifah wasn't my favorite person, but I couldn't stand this nigga. He reached his hand out for a shake, but I left it there hanging.

He ran his hand through his hair, "Oh it's like that I see. It's cool, though. You're here and that's all that matters."

"Fuck you!" He laughed, unphased by my derogatory response.

"Tough guy, I like that." He smirked; it took everything in me not to smack the shit out this pale fool.

"Terrance, let me show you something." Latifah stepped in. She walked off motioning for me to follow her, I stood there for a second staring him down. His stupid smirk remained plastered on his face. I couldn't wait to make that shit a permanent look. I smirked at the thought.

As told by Malcolm

Essence looked so beautiful getting ready for her launch. I was so proud of her. She was so strong, after all the shit she's been through. What I loved about her the most is that she never let it show. I could tell she was anxious, but that was expected. After all, she was showcasing her work in a new city. Back in New York she had a buzz already. They were familiar with what she could do.

I could feel my dick rise as I watched her ass from behind. Essence's curves were perfection. She made sure her make-up was flawless and every strand of hair was where it needed to be. She could be draped in rags and still capture all the attention.

Hopefully, tonight I will be able to relax. Hopefully we both will be able to.

As told by Essence

My nerves were getting the best of me as I was getting ready for the party tonight. So many thoughts crossed my mind. Would everyone like the new *Jo Nova*? What about Malcolm and Latifah in the same room? How in the hell was I going to pull that off?

"You look amazing." Malcolm came up behind me and kissed my neck.

"You think so?" I spun around for him. As he watched my curves, his eyes lit up.

He whispered in my ear, "I can't wait to bring you back home and rip that dress off you."

"You know how much this cost?" I joked. We both shared a laugh. We needed that. The undisclosed tension between us was thick, nothing a little laughter couldn't try to mend.

After giving myself another once over in the mirror, we headed for the party.

The car ride was silent as Malcolm held my hand. We pulled up to Stone and the line was ridiculous. For this to be an invite only event the crowd was poppin'. *Jackson & Jackson* really brought the town out.

Malcolm opened my door and I stepped out of the car. He handed the valet his keys and led me to the door. I felt like everybody in line was staring at us as we walked ahead of them. I glanced at Malcolm who was smirking just enough for his dimples to show. That made me smile in return.

Chino, one of the guards from *Jackson & Jackson,* was at the door.

"Aye, Essence." He reached for a hug.

"Hey Chino," I replied giving him a hug.

"And you must be Malcolm." Chino stretched out his hand.

Malcolm welcomed Chino's hand, stating proudly, "Yes, I am." I rolled my eyes at Malcolm's cockiness as Chino stepped aside and let us in.

Stone was already a nice spot, but the way the event team put this together was dope! The yellow accent around the room screamed *Jackson & Jackson*. It was just as many people inside as it was outside. That was quite impressive.

"Beautiful," My body tensed up at her voice. I turned to see Latifah, standing behind us. She was dressed in a yellow laced dress, which complemented her skin so stunningly. My heart skipped a beat as the guy I love and the woman I was lusting over stood side by side.

"Hey, Latifah…you look, nice. And everything here is amazing." I finally spoke.

"Yes, I agree." Malcolm agreed making his presence known.

"Thank you. And thanks for coming Malcolm."

"No doubt. I'll do anything for my

girl." Malcolm grabbed my waist, pulling me in close to him kissing my cheek. I smiled. The look on Latifah's face was one of jealousy, but only I could see.

"Well," she spoke again, "won't you two head over there to the VIP section, drinks on me." Latifah pointed to our area and Malcolm led the way. I couldn't help but look back at Latifah who was of course still looking with her intense eyes.

"Aye, my boy." Malcolm greeted Terrance who was already seated.

"Hey, wassup." Terrance stood up, dapping Malcolm up and giving me a hug. "Hey sis."

"You look sharp. And you on time." I joked.

"Power of the pussy." Malcolm laughed. He was referring to Latifah. Terrance giggled a tad bit, but not much.

"Everything okay Terrance?" I asked.

"Yeah, yeah. I'm good." He stumbled. I could tell that was far from the truth, but I let him be.

"Can I get you anything?" A waitress came over to us, she was staring Malcolm down.

"I'll take, a vodka and cranberry and a shot of cognac." I ordered for us. She looked my way embarrassed without making eye contact. She flashed a half smile before walking away.

"You see the way she was gawking at you?" I turned to Malcolm and asked.

He laughed, "What? She was doing her job."

"Yeah, she was trying to do you." I rolled my eyes and laughed.

"You jealous, eh?" He teased.

"Never that, you mine." I said with confidence. We laughed a little more. And before we knew it, she was back with our drinks. She set out drinks down in front of us.

"Is that all?" She asked. She finally looked at me instead of Malcolm. I guess she got the hint.

"We're good." She went to walk away. As she turned, Terrance was getting up and almost knocked her over.

"Oh sorry, excuse me." She apologized to him. Terrance shook his head and walked away.

"Hey, don't I know you?" I asked her.

"I'm sorry, I don't think we've met." She hurried on. I know that girl from somewhere. I can't quite put my finger on it. The fear that resonated from her was very familiar to me.

Malcolm looked at me smiling and shook his head. He must've thought I was trying to intimidate her from the little stunt she pulled earlier, but that was not the case.

As told by Terrance

As I waked off I overheard Essence ask the waitress if she knew her. Once she came out the VIP section I had to catch up with her. I grabbed her by the arm and pulled her to the back of the bar.

"Heyy, what are you doing?" She screeched.

"What's your name?" I asked.

"Lydia." She answered without hesitation. The fear in her eyes confirmed my next question without it being asked.

"You work for Latifah?" She shook her head yes. Tears forming in her eyes.

"How do you know Essence?" She looked at me without responding. I grabbed her arm tighter until she spoke.

"I don't. I don't know her. I ran into her one day at a photoshoot."

"A photoshoot?" I was confused.

"Yes, I modeled a few garments for *Jackson & Jackson*." My blood boiled as I tried to put pieces together.

"Don't go back near her."

"But, Latif…" I shot her a look and she put her head down.

"Okay." I finally let go of her, leaving her standing there rubbing her arm where my hands just laid.

I shook my head. I wanted Latifah's head on a platter. She begged me not to say anything to Essence about the bullshit she was doing, but yet she was bringing the bullshit around her. I stood at the bar, scoping the scene.

I spotted Tara and Kisha out making their rounds. They played the role as bartenders dressed in white leotards. I looked around at all the bartenders, some familiar from when we first stepped in Stone, all in white leotards. I had to admit, Latifah was smart. It was the easiest way to keep track of all the girls and no one would have a suspicion of what was going down.

I peeped the bidders too. They all wore a white handkerchief in their left pocket. No matter what they had on. They blended in with the crowd as if they were really interested in some damn magazine. All they wanted was for the clock to strike midnight and all their perverted wishes would come true. I laughed; the shit wasn't funny at all, but my revenge would be.

"Having a good time?" Latifah came up and stood close to me. I had to admit, she looked good as fuck in this yellow dress.

She ran her fingers across my chest, grinning. My breathing sped up. I was face to face with the enemy, but my dick was standing at attention for her. She looked down at it and licked her lips.

"He don't hate me as much as you do." She kissed me on the lips before walking away. Latifah left me there looking stupid. I fixated my eyes on her, as I watched her work the crowd. She got mad love from everywhere. When I spotted ol' boy come up to her, my dick went limp. I didn't expect him to be here.

That wasn't part of the plan.

In full fury, I walked over to them. He was shaking hands with everyone, with an innocent smile on his face. Latifah turned just in time to see me coming.

"Hey Vincent. There's someone I would like you to meet." I stopped dead in my tracks. These mutherfuckers were putting on a show.

"The pleasure is all mine, Latifah." He reached out his hand to shake mine. I was hesitant to take his hand, until Latifah shrugged me. Everyone in the little circle was staring at me. I took his hand.

"Terrance." I stated.

"Terrance, I've heard such good things about you. Latifah can't stop talking about you at work." *Work,* I thought, while everyone laughed.

"This is Maria and Franky."

"Nice to meet you." They both spoke in unison. Maria batted her eyes at me and for a second I could've swore, Franky did too.

"Vincent here is the brains behind *Jackson & Jackson.*" Latifah bragged. *The brains? Oh, hell nah, he knows Essence too.*

I nodded my head. I had to find a way to get out of this conversation before I lost it. I had to play this one smart; with all this new information I just gained, I couldn't execute my plan tonight like I planned to.

"Look, it was nice meeting ya'll, but I'm about to head over to my fam." I didn't wait for them to excuse me. I headed back over to VIP. My first thought was to let Malcolm in on this shit. I needed to keep it real with him and let him know what was really going on. There is strength in numbers and I know Malcolm would have my back.

As told by Essence
Malcolm and I were enjoying our night

together and everyone else seemed to be enjoying their night as well.

Terrance finally rejoined us with Latifah on his heels.

"Ayo, Malcolm can I holla at you for a second?" Malcolm looked at me as if to ask for permission. I nodded my head, letting him know I would be fine without him.

"Wait," Latifah said alarmingly, "um, Vincent wants to come over to say hello." Latifah motioned for him.

"Heyy Essence my star of the night. What are you doing in the corner all night? And this must be Malcolm?" Vincent talked non-stopped. I laughed at his enthusiasm. He was always so overjoyed.

"Yes, this is Malcolm, and his best friend Terrance." I introduced the two.

"We met." Terrance stated coldly.

"Yeah, yeah. We have. Anyway, get up out this corner and go mingle. I'll keep the boys here some company. Run along."

"But," I started.

"Go head baby. Do your thing." Malcolm encouraged. I kissed him on the cheek and left with Latifah. She held my hands down the stairs, as if I couldn't walk on my own. But, I didn't mind at all. Her touch was delicate.

Latifah pranced around the room, introducing me to everyone. She boasted about me so much, I was flattered. I didn't even have to speak much, she acted as my spokesperson. It was nice meeting everyone, but I was overwhelmed. And my cheeks burned from the smile I had plastered on my face.

"You know a lot of people." I said to Latifah when we finally had a moment to ourselves. She didn't entertain my statement much, she just bopped her head in agreeance.

"I'm going to the ladies' room."
Latifah brushed past me and walked
towards the bathroom. I had no other
choice but to follow her. She peeked
inside to each stall making sure it was
vacant before proceeding back to the
door to lock it. My heart sped up as I
stood in the same spot unable to move.

"Latifah, look." I stuttered, "I don't
know."

"There's nothing for you to know."
Latifah spoke nonchalantly. She traced
my bare shoulder with her fingertips.
Goosebumps formed immediately.
Latifah's soft hands stroked my arm,
tracing the bumps my arm possessed. I
felt my head drop, as my lips parted and
my breathing sped up.

A soft moan left my lips answering
Latifah's touch. Latifah led my fingers
into her mouth as she sucked my middle
finger. My panties were dripping, my
mind racing, but it was out of my control.

It was like she casted a spell on me. Latifah moved from my right hand to my left hand with the same precision.

She then gripped my breast in her hands. She gently squeezed them both at the same time, taking her time fingering my hard nipples. My legs got weak at her touch,

Latifah was biting down on her lip and I mirrored her image. She continued to grope my breast, leaning in to kiss my neck. Her kisses were warm, causing the hairs on the back of my neck to stand at attention.

Latifah guided me to the sink counter. She turned me around and spread my arms across the mirror. Her lips continued to touch my neck as her hands made their way to my hips. My hips slowly moved, matching her energy. Latifah's fingers moved over to my freshly waxed pussy and they began to dance on my clit. Louder moans left my throat as I stared at our faces in the mirror.

"Essence," Latifah yelled, "Essence!" I snapped out of my day dream. "You coming?"

"Yeah, yeah." I gathered my thoughts together as I followed her to the bathroom.

As told by Malcolm

The scene at Stone was lit. *Jackson & Jackson* really showed out, all for my baby. We were bringing in this new year the right way. Terrance and I kicked it with Vincent a little bit. Terrance was uninterested in dude, but he was cool with me. When he finally stepped away I turned to Terrance.

"So, what you had to talk to me about? Tell me you found something on that Crespo shit."

"Nah, not yet. But look man, I can't really tell you much right now. Just know this shit ain't all what it's cracked up to be." I looked at Terrance funny.

"Man, what you talking bout? You had too many drinks tonight?" I started to laugh, but the look on Terrance's face said that it wasn't the right time for it. I leaned in closer to Terrance and he leaned in as well.

"Vincent and Lat…"

"Ladies and gentlemen!" Vincent interrupted Terrance, "thanks for coming out tonight. As always, I am delighted that you all came. You all look nice. Not as good as me, of course." A sea of laughter filled the club. "I would like you all to meet Miss Essence Brown. Essence? Essence? Where are you?"

I searched the crowd, until I found my baby, walking over to where Vincent was. Her face was glowing at the recognition.

"Essence, here, came from New York. She ran a very chic magazine out there called *Jo Nova*. Just a few months back,

we welcomed Essence at *Jackson &
Jackson* and she has been a pleasure to
work with. Some of you may be counting
down to a new year, but here at *Jackson &
Jackson* we are counting down to a new
edition to our family." The crowd roared
and whistled.

"Let the countdown begin!"

"Ten…Nine…Eight…Seven…Six….
Five…Four…Three…Two…One…….
Happy New Year!" The crowd screamed
as the magazine cover was unveiled. The
crowd screamed even louder. The cover
displayed Essence. She was in total
shock. I made my way through the
crowd, leaving Terrance where he was.

I stood by Essence as she had tears in
her eyes. She hugged Latifah and Vincent
before turning to me.

"Malcolm, I had no idea I was on the
cover." She awed.

"You look great, baby." I cheered her
on. Hugging her tight. Everyone around

us was blowing horns and whistles. Although, it was part of the New Year festivities, it felt like it was our moment in love that prompted it.

My baby was happy, which is all I ever wanted. Let this year stay this way.

CHAPTER 8

As told by Essence

"It was just beautiful." I described to Ma and Unique over the phone. I couldn't wait to call them to let them know how the party went.

"I'm so proud of you sister." Unique congratulated me.

"Thank you sissy!" I cooed, "You're up next."

"Speaking of next, can I come live with you?" Unique whined. Her voice began to fade as Ma took over.

"Well, baby. I'm glad that you're adjusting well."

"Ma, what was that about?"

"What?" She acted as if she didn't just hear what Unique just asked me.

"What's going on out there?"

"Nothing, Chile. We're fine." I could hear Unique in the background, but couldn't make out what she was saying.

"Let me talk to Unique, Ma." Instead of putting Unique on the phone, the line disconnected. I looked at my phone to make sure it wasn't poor service, but it was clear that Ma had hung up. I called back and immediately got the voicemail.

I let out a sigh. Loud enough to wake Malcolm up.

"Everything good Essence?" He questioned, wiping the sleep out of his eye.

"I just talked to Ma and something isn't right."

"She okay? Unique okay? What is it?" Malcolm sat up and fired off questions.

I shook my head. "Malcolm, I don't

know what's going on, but Unique asked to come move with me. Ma pretended like she didn't hear her. And when I asked what was going on, she hung up on me."

"Did you try calling back?"

"Yes, Malcolm. It went straight to voicemail."

"Maybe her phone died. I'm sure it's nothing but teenage girl drama." Malcolm attempted to cheer me up. He was right. I was probably overreacting. If something was going on, Unique would have been called me. Even with the age gap and distance between us, we had a tight-niched bond.

"You always know what to say." I kissed Malcolm.

"I do, don't I?" He teased, kissing my neck.

"Umm hmm." I muttered as his warm kisses excited me. Malcolm planted warm kisses all over my body.

"I'm so proud of you baby." He whispered in between kisses. His soft lips felt like silk against my skin, as he imbedded a trail of kisses down to my navel.

"You always know what to do."

"I do, don't I?" He teased again, this time getting closer to my clit.

"Ohhh yeaah." I managed to say as he tongue kissed my pearl. Each time his tongue flicked up or down, my hips moved with him. He didn't need any guidance, but it didn't stop my hands from gripping his head keeping him closer. The grind in my hips matched the effort in his stroke until I almost reached my climax. Then he stopped.

Malcolm looked at me and smiled as I struggled to hold my breath. I was so close to cumin all over his juicy lips. Malcolm licked his thumb and started rubbing my clit in small slow circles.

"Stop teasing me," I screamed, even

though it felt good.

"You want me to stop?" Malcolm removed his thumb leaving my clit pulsating.

"Noo, baby please don't."

Malcolm laughed, "I thought so." He then dived face first between my legs. My legs tensed up as I squeezed his head, lifting my ass off the bed. Malcolm forcefully pushed me back down. I tried to run from him, but he held me down. I waved the white flag, it was clear that I was the weaker one and it was not a battle I could win. I surrendered to him, releasing all I had in me. He smiled at his sweet tasting victory.

As told by Malcolm

"Malcolm, if Hill Homes don't work out, you could always be a chef." Essence sat back in the bed, rubbing her belly. Morning head and breakfast in bed was a perfect combination. I loved cooking for

Essence. I loved pleasing her, as a whole.

"Thanks." I chuckled.

"Something wrong?" Essence asked.

I wiped my mouth before speaking, "Did you think Terrance was acting a little different last night?" I wanted to make sure it wasn't just me.

"I'm glad you said it first. I noticed he was a little reserved."

"Yeah, me too. He wanted to speak to me about some shit too. Something about Vincent and Latifah."

"What about them?"

"I don't know, he didn't get a chance to tell me. We got interrupted. But on the real, Latifah a little too friendly with you."

Essence laughed nervously.

"I'm serious. You may not see it, but she acts like she feeling you."

"Nah, that's just how she is."

"Yeah, okay." Essence couldn't tell me she didn't notice the way Latifah interacted with her. Just by the way her body language changed when Latifah was around, was enough to convince me my speculations were correct. I wasn't a jealous type of nigga, but I will fuck a mutherfucker up over my baby. Nigga or bitch.

"I'm bout to hit Terrance up, to see what's good with him. You gonna be okay here?"

The look on Essence's face was like she was in deep thought, "I'll be here when you get back." She forced a smile. I flashed a fake smile too, before getting in the shower.

I replayed last night's conversation with Terrance in my head. We still haven't found out what's up with Crespo and the niggas that tried to kill me. Now he was talking some oh other shit about Vincent and Latifah. Vincent seemed cool to me each time I was around him. Latifah been sketchy from jump, so hearing her name wasn't a surprise to me.

I was even starting to question Terrance. He was my man a hundred grand, but the way he been moving lately was giving me a funny feeling. Regardless, it points back to Latifah. Once he met that bitch was when I noticed the change in him.

"Call Pablo." I called out to my voice command.

"Calling Pablo."

"Yoo Malcolm, what's good nigga?" He answered. It's been a while since I spoke to him, but it was all love.

"Ain't shit man, wassup with you?"

"You know man, just trying take care of the family."

"I hear that. I hear that. Yo I need you to check on something for me."

"What you need?"

"I need all the information you can

find on
a Latifah Washington."

"Bet."

"Bet." If there was one person I knew that
could find out who Latifah was, I know Pablo was the man for it. I couldn't leave it up to Terrance and his boys. I needed to keep this one under wraps. Especially if the bitch was as dirty as I thought she was. And if she wasn't, I'd leave it alone. But I had to find out what I could, from every angle.

I slowed down as I pulled onto the street of Hill Homes, blasting my music, preparing to receive whatever information Terrance had for me.

Boom! I got rear-ended causing my head to jerk forward. I looked in my rearview mirror to see what the fuck was going on.

"What the fuck!" I said out loud. Behind me was a black Suburban. I hit the gas trying to dodge the next hit, but I failed.

Boom! My head hit the steering wheel from the force. My head dazed, as I gathered myself together and swerved lanes. The Suburban followed me getting close enough to ram me again, but I sped up leaving enough slack. Whoever was driving was quick because every lead I got was short lived. They were right on my bumper.

Cars honked at us, as we sped through Chicago streets thinking,this can't be happening right now. I had a target on my back without even knowing who was behind it.

I finally got a big enough lead and lost the Suburban. I laughed looking in the rearview mirror. I dialed Terrance's phone and of course he didn't answer. His voicemail came on and I hung up. I dialed the office phone and that phone kept ringing to the answering machine.

"This nigga man." I said.

Crash! My head whipped forward and back as I got hit hard enough to send me into a tree. My airbag went off and I could feel blood trickling from my forehead. I tasted blood in my mouth. Broken glass was all over the front seat. I climbed out my car and the next thing I know, I woke up in a hospital bed.

"Malcolm, baby. I'm here." Essence's beautiful face was the first thing I saw when I opened my eyes.

"Nurse! Nurse! His eyes are open." Essence called out as a young, tall white lady with red hair came in. I tried to get up, but couldn't move. I heard beeping noises from the machines all around me. I went to speak, but nothing came out.

"No, baby. Don't try to speak." Essence touched my hand gently. Even in my condition she was here, loving me, the definition of unconditional love.

I looked around the room. Terrance

was there sitting in a chair by the window with his head in his hands.

I reached my arm up to point at Terrance. Essence turned to him and called his name. Terrance looked up. His eyes were bloodshot red as if he was crying.

"My bad, G. I'm gonna find out who did this shit to you. This is getting out of hand, I got my peeps on it and I ain't sleeping until we do." All I could do was nod my head. Essence looked at me worried.

"Terrance, please tell me what's going on." She begged.

Terrance looked at me for the okay before he filled her in on what was happening.

"Oh my God!" Essence's hands covered her opened mouth. Her beautiful face showed fear, just as I knew she would. This is why I didn't want to tell her.

"Terrance, do you know who this could be? It's not…" Essence didn't need to finish her question. We already knew what she was thinking.

"Nah. But, don't worry about it sis. I got it handled." I nodded my head again, agreeing with Terrance. Ain't no question he would handle it. The real question was when? Again, I called and he wasn't there. This was nothing like Terrance, he has been my right hand since I met him. No doubt. I never had to question his loyalty, but something was getting in the way. The fact that he wasn't telling leads me to believe he's either embarrassed or he's doing some fucked up shit. Whichever it was, it didn't feel good.

As told by Terrance

Whomever was behind Malcolm being followed, was definitely a part of this car accident. It was no doubt that whoever it was, wanted Malcolm dead. I honestly forgot about this Crespo shit. It was easy to forget shit that wasn't happening directly to you. Yes, it affected me, but with all this shit going on with Latifah and Vincent, I had no time to think about nothing else.

As I watched Malcolm lay up in that hospital bed, with Essence at his side, my heart got heavy. It wasn't supposed to happen like this. We were supposed to be celebrating a new year, new beginnings, new money, but instead we were hurting.

It was only a matter of time before, everyone would feel my wrath.

CHAPTER 9

As told by Essence

I haven't stopped crying since I got the call from the hospital that Malcolm was in a car accident. Here I was thinking it was just an accident, but Terrance let me know that wasn't the case. I can't believe Malcolm was keeping this from me, but I understand why he did. He was attempting to protect me and ended up getting hurt himself.

I couldn't bear to look at Malcolm in that bed. I've never seen him this weak before and it was hurting my damn soul. I couldn't imagine a life without

Malcolm. I wouldn't imagine it. I'm glad that he is making it through.

Terrance was fucked up over this situation too. When I called him, all he said was "on my way" before hanging up. He got to the hospital in record timing. He didn't speak much, the most he said was explaining all the things Malcolm had been experiencing over the last few weeks.

I spent day in and day out with Malcolm. His accident was all over the news. Detectives visited, frequently asking questions. Malcolm's story remained the same. He didn't see who it was, he didn't know who was behind it. That didn't stop them from coming up and trying to get information. What was Malcolm going to say? I killed a dude in New York for kidnapping my girlfriend and now I think his people are after me? They would've locked him up so quick without taking his health into consideration.

Terrance visited faithfully as well. He updated Malcolm on business, but every time it came to Crespo they asked me to step out. I didn't put up a fight. I know they tried their best to keep me out of the mix, but I was going to find out what was going on. And I knew right where to start.

"Essence, what are you doing here?' Latifah asked as she opened the door to see me standing outside.

"I'm sorry for coming unannounced." I dropped my head and Latifah lifted it back up.

"You've been crying." Latifah grabbed my hand and led me into her house.

"How's everything going, beautiful?" Latifah and I sat on her couch as she looked at me with a face full of concern.

"Malcolm…" is all I got out before I burst into tears. Latifah pulled me close as I cried on her shoulder. She ran her fingers through my hair as I sobbed.

"It's going to be okay. This will pass." Latifah whispered.

"You sure?" I looked to Latifah for reassurance.

Instead of replying, she kissed me. Her kiss was sweeter than our first kiss, there was no liquor clouding our judgement, it was pure chemistry. I reached up and grabbed Latifah's face and kissed her back.

"You sure?" She broke our kiss to ask. And without saying a word, I showed her I was. I laid back on the couch and watched Latifah climb on top of me.

We kissed as if we were long time lovers, so in sync with one another. Our hands were all over each other, gently but at the same time aggressively. She started undressing me and I let her.

I laid on Latifah's couch with nothing but my underwear and bra on. She inspected my body, up and down, licking her lips. She began to undress herself and I stopped her.

"Let me." I whispered, Latifah stopped fumbling with the buttons on her silk shirt and let me take over. She massaged my head again. My eyes rolled back making it hard for me to continue my task.

Once Latifah's silk pajama shirt was off, she yanked my hair back, causing me to let out a loud moan.

"You like that?" She asked seductively.

I licked my lips as I pulled on her pajama shorts. Latifah was wearing nothing underneath. Her slim chocolate body was glistening with gold shimmer.

Latifah's breast were small and perky, her pussy was neatly trimmed. Latifah kissed my chest as she let my titties out my bra and begin sucking them. My nipples were already hard and my pussy started dripping. She took her time on each titty equally, just as I dreamed. I closed my eyes enjoying her tender loving care.

Latifah began kissing my stomach and licking between each one she planted on me. Her tongue traced my panty line as she got closer to my hot box. I lifted my ass off the couch a little as Latifah pulled down my thong with her teeth. Once they were down far enough, she massaged my clit.

It was clear Latifah had some experience at this. She answered every cue my body gave off. It was as if she knew what I wanted and how I wanted it. After all, she was a woman too.

Latifah replaced her fingertips with her tongue and it nearly sent me over the edge, literally. I wanted her to continue, but my natural reaction was to move away. Her tongue did numbers as my legs began to shake.

"Ohhhh." I cried out as I climaxed. Latifah lapped up every bit of my juices.

Latifah smiled at me and licked her lips. "You taste better than I thought."

I pushed Latifah down on her back and sucked her bottom lip. She let out soft moans as I caressed her breast. I took one after another into my warm mouth, making her call out.

"Yesss, beautiful." Latifah called. I loved how she called me beautiful. It felt so sincere.

I traced her midline down to her clit. I stopped mid-action as I realized I've never tasted anyone's pussy juices besides my own, off someone else's lips.

"Go with the flow." Latifah whispered, she could sense my hesitancy.

What the hell, we already came this far. She went out her way to please me and I had to return the favor. I wanted to return the favor. Now that I had my chance, I was going to take it.

I parted Latifah's lips with my fingers and I vibrated my tongue against her clit.

She immediately grabbed my head and started thrusting her hips forward. Her body's reaction was enough to let me know I was doing it right. I licked up and down and around her clit. My pussy began to drip at the way she was responding. I inserted two fingers inside her and circled them in and out.

"Damn, beautiful." Latifah moaned.

"You like that?" I asked seductively, imitating her from earlier.

"Oh yes. Um hm." Latifah answered as I continued to please her.

"I'm cumin', beautiful." And just as she finished her sentence she came long and hard.

I tasted every bit of her as her legs tensed up. I took out my fingers and made her lick them. I laid between her legs as she breathed heavily.

My intentions were to come find out about Terrance's behavior and how it could be related to Malcolm's accident. I accomplished none of that, but one thing on my to-do list was complete. The thought of Malcolm made me realize what I had just done. My first sexual encounter with a woman turned out to be one I wanted to relive. Malcolm held my heart, but Latifah was holding my body hostage.

"What's wrong beautiful?" Latifah came out the bathroom.

"Nothing."

Latifah stepped closer and got in bed next to me, "I won't tell, if you don't." Latifah began to stroke my arm. I rubbed my thumb across her cheek.

Knock! Knock!

"Who's there?" Latifah called out.

"Aye, its Terrance. Can I come in?" Latifah and I looked at each other in a panic.

"What's he doing here?" I whispered. I hopped out of bed, scrambling to put back on my clothes.

"I don't know." She whispered back. Fuck! The last thing I needed was Terrance seeing me here. Latifah waited until I was dressed and went to open the door and Terrance rushed in.

"Oh, hey sis. I thought you were up at the hospital."

"I, um was just leaving."

"Oh ok." I tried to see if his body language gave away anything. He knew Latifah and I were cool. My company here was harmless. Right?

"Latifah, I'll call you later, so we can um…finish up things." I started to stutter again. Latifah gave me a goodbye hug. I closed my eyes and got a good whiff of her natural body scent. A rush of nerve impulses went through my body. The hug seemed to last an eternity. I rushed to the car and wanted to cry.

As told by Terrance

Latifah must've had a death wish. I

warned that bitch, to stay away from Essence. There was no way they needed to communicate with each other outside of work.

"Terrance, don't be coming over my fucking house unannounced." Latifah spat, walking away. I grabbed the back of Latifah's neck and forced her against the wall.

"What the fuck are you doing?" She immediately started crying.

"What the fuck are you doing? I told you to stay away from her."

"I know. I tried, but..."

"Ain't no more fucking buts."

"You're going to regret this." She managed to say.

I grit my teeth, "Bitch, you're going to regret ever fucking me. I'm not your bitch. You or Vincent. I am out of your fuckin sex trade."

"No, you're not. We will see what your fat ass mama thinks about this."

I didn't think twice as I smacked Latifah down to the ground. Her words burned like venom. She could've said anything else, but mentioning Ma Dukes again, was out of pocket.

She laughed with a mouth full of blood as she spit the blood out, "you can smack me all you want, but Sheila will get way worse."

"Cut your fucking threats." She stopped laughing when she noticed I wasn't moved by anymore of her threats towards Mama. I began to laugh and she stared at me crazily.

I pulled out my phone and shoved it in her face. Her tears returned as she sobbed.

"What the fuck did you do to him?" She screamed. I laughed louder.

"Terrrrrraaaaaance!" She yelled, but I continued laughing. She looked so pitiful sitting on the floor hysterical.

"I warned you. You didn't want to

listen. Stay the fuck away from my family. I'm out." My job here was done, but not until I hawked spit on her. I could hear her sobbing still as I walked down the steps.

I smiled, satisfied. Now, it was time to pay Vincent a visit.

CHAPTER 10

As told by Malcolm

How the fuck did I end up in this situation? Laid up in a fucking hospital bed for seven days, doctors and nurses in and out my room. To make matters worse, the fucking pigs kept coming up to my room questioning me. This shit is awful. The doc said my arm was broke in three different places. My ribs were bruised and I had a minor concussion. As fucked up as it sounds, I'm just happy to have made it out alive. I lost a lot of blood. They gave me two blood transfusions the first night because I lost so much blood. Now they were monitoring my blood count. I could barely sleep at night. I tossed and turned trying to figure out who was behind this hit and how I was going to get my revenge.

Essence stayed right at the hospital with me, I watched my baby laying in the recliner next to my bed. I didn't mean for her to find out like this. Shit, I didn't want her to find out at all, but after this accident, she needed to know. She needed to be mindful of her surroundings, just in case these mutherfuckers tried to pull something on her. I was ready to kill at the thought of Essence in danger again. I was going to find out who was behind this, before things got any more crazy.

"Mr. Hill." My doc entered the room.

"Wassup doc." I greeted him.

"You my man, it looks like you're clear to go home. Your labs are back to normal and I don't see another reason why you'd have to stay."

"Thank God."

"I'll put in your discharge order so your nurse can get you up out of here."

"No doubt." I reached out my right hand to shake his, he shook my hand and exited the room. I reached for my cell to call Essence, she had stepped out this morning to handle business. I called a few times before she picked up.

"Everything alright?" She finally answered.

"Everything's great. They letting a nigga up outta here."

"Yayy!" She screamed through the phone, I jumped back because she was so loud, and, standing in my doorway.

The nurse came in to give me my discharge instructions and I was out of there. We stopped at the pharmacy to grab my meds before reaching home. To my surprise, Aunt Carol and Ms. Sheila were in the driveway, awaiting my arrival. I made sure neither one of them stepped foot in the hospital to see me. They didn't like that decision, but they respected it. I guess they couldn't wait another minute to see me.

"Oh, my baby." Aunt Carol and Ms. Sheila bombarded me as I got out the car. Essence laughed.

"What ya'll doing here?" I spoke grimacing. My ribs were sore as hell. Every time I talked, coughed, or moved too quick, I felt the agonizing pain. Their hugs didn't make it any better.

"What you think we doing here?" Ms. Sheila sassed me with her hands on her hips. Terrance got his looks from his Mama for sure. Ms. Sheila was about 5'7'. Her skin was the color of caramel. At 60 years old, she lived up to black don't crack. She was gorgeous. Ms. Sheila, undeniably, gave Terrance his grit. I knew better than to try them, but I wanted to stay low from their wrath.

"Ms. Sheila, Aunt Carol, I ain't mean nothing by that. I don't want ya'll seeing me like this.

Aunt Carol moved in close to me, "Malcolm, don't be silly. You know we gonna take care of you. I made a promise to yo' mama and the Lord."

"And I'm just stuck." Ms. Sheila joked. I chuckled a bit, causing even more pain. I grabbed my left side with my right hand.

"Baby, don't laugh. Don't even talk," Aunt Carol ordered, "Sheila, cut all that foolishness. You see my baby in pain. Aunt Carol was a splitting image of Mama. They could've passed for twins, if Aunt Carol didn't always make it known that she was the big sister. I've always saw Mama in Aunt Carol, although Aunt Carol was stricter than Mama ever was. Aunt Carol played no games at all. I guess you can say, that's where I learned my 'don't take shit' attitude from.

Ms. Sheila rolled her eyes at Aunt Carol. These two were such characters. Their personalities were both so big, it was hard to contain them. They had mad love for each other, but weren't afraid to tell the other one how they felt. Not a lot of women could take their honesty, but they had each other and they were fine with that.

Ms. Sheila rubbed her head, "I'm sorry Malcolm. I was trying to lighten the mood. Like Carol said, don't you worry. We gonna take care of you." They both grabbed an arm leading me into the house. Essence grabbed the bags out the car before coming to unlock the front door.

"Where's Terrance?" Aunt Carol asked.

"Hmm." Ms. Sheila rolled her eyes at the mentioning of Terrance's name and walked into the living room.

"What the hell you huffing and puffing for?" Aunt Carol looked at Ms. Sheila.

"That damn Terrance been rubbing me the wrong way. The boy is off. He's not himself."

"He's probably sick of you." Aunt Carol laughed, but Ms. Sheila didn't crack a smile. I looked at Essence, we knew exactly what she was talking about though.

"It ain't funny Carol. He's been acting real suspicious. I hope he ain't doing nothing stupid to land his behind in prison again. Any time he come over, he's always on the damn phone whispering to somebody. And then he takes off."

Ms. Sheila became serious again, "well did you ask him what was going on?"

"Yes, I did. But he told me it was work related," Ms. Sheila looked to me. "I know you two just closed that Jones

Place deal. So, I left him alone. If there's one thing I know about that boy, it was to leave him be, when he said leave him be."

"Yeah. Jones Place has been hectic. You know, getting everything in order and making sure we're on the right track. Terrance been putting in a lot of work for Hill Homes." I added to Terrance's story. I didn't need to alarm Ms. Sheila that I witnessed the same behavior she had.

"If it's that bad, it ain't worth it." Aunt Carol started to preach. Ms. Sheila co-signed everything Aunt Carol said. They knew how much Jones Place meant to us, so this preaching was falling on deaf ears.

"Essence, we gon' stay here as long as you need us to help out." Aunt Carol stated.

"Thank you." Essence replied.

"Nah. Nah. It's cool Aunt Carol. We appreciate the offer though." Essence was fully capable of handling things around here.

"The hell you ain't? You spent a week laid up in the hospital bed, ya both tired and need help." Aunt Carol growled. Ms. Sheila shook her head at Aunt Carol's rant. I couldn't help but laugh at them again, despite the pain I felt from the pressure.

"Go sit down somewhere. I'll fix you something to eat. Them young kids in that hospital can't cook." I looked for Ms. Sheila to roll her eyes at Aunt Carol's comment, but she shook her head and agreed. Essence followed them both into the kitchen.

As told by Essence

"Everything okay?" Ms. Sheila asked.

"Yeah, yeah." I answered.

"It don't seem like it."

"Sheila, leave the girl alone." Aunt Carol stepped in to save me. I'm glad she did, my guilty conscience was hovering over my head and it was like she saw it for herself.

"Work keeping you busy?" Ms. Sheila asked. Aunt Carol nudged her on the side.

"What?" Ms. Sheila screwed her face up at Aunt Carol.

"You stay in folk's business." Aunt Carol told her.

I giggled. "It's okay Aunt Carol. Yes, work has been very busy."

"I see." Ms. Sheila responded. I walked away to go check on Malcolm.

"Will you stop butting your nose in people business?" I heard Aunt Carol whisper to Ms. Sheila.

"Malcolm, is my business. Don't you think she acting a little strange? I love her to death, but something is up. Watch I tell ya." I didn't catch Aunt Carol's response. Ms. Sheila was right, something was up, but it was not the place nor time to expose it.

"Malcolm." I went over to hug him. I began to cry. I cried because I almost lost him and if he were to find out what I did, I could potentially still lose him.

"I'm scared, Malcolm." I admitted.

Malcolm wiped my tears, "Don't be scared."

"What if they come back?" I questioned.

"Shhhh. Don't worry, baby." Malcolm and I held each other as tight as his sore body would allow us.

"Food is ready." Aunt Carol yelled out to us, interrupting our intimate moment. I wiped my eyes and helped Malcolm up off the couch and into the dining room.

Aunt Carol and Ms. Sheila sparked most of the conversation. I could tell Malcolm's mind was searching for answers, plotting revenge and replaying scenarios. My mind was also clouded. After we ate, I helped Aunt Carol clear the table. Ms. Sheila helped Malcolm upstairs.

"You and Malcolm alright?" Aunt Carol wasted no time. After telling Ms. Sheila to stay out our business, here she was butting in.

"We're fine." I kept it short and sweet.

"Fine?" Aunt Carol replied, but the look on her face said she wasn't buying it.

"Essence, I love you. You're such a talented and damn good woman. You make sure you take care of my Malcolm. I'm not trying to get in you all's business, but I sensed something was off at dinner.

I remained silent as I washed the dishes.

"You don't have to tell me. It's best you keep your problems between ya'll two anyway. But you make sure ya'll work it out. You young folks give up on love so easy. One little thing goes wrong, ya'll be ready to throw it all away. Ain't nothing in life easy and if it's worth it, you'll fight for it. Stay honest and keep the communication line open." It was like Aunt Carol could see right through me, just as Ms. Sheila did. I took everything she said into consideration. After all, she was right.

CHAPTER 11

As told by Terrance

Since Latifah was put in her place, I could focus on the real task at hand. And that was finding out who the fuck boys were that were trying to kill Malcolm.

"What you got for me?" I pulled up on my young boys.

"You know we got you, Unc." Lil L spoke up. You could call him the leader of the pack. He made sure everybody stayed on they shit.

Lil L handed me an envelope. I couldn't wait to see what was inside of it, but I figured I should wait for Malcolm.

It took longer than expected, but what was a couple more minutes?

I handed Lil L a stack, "for your trouble."

"Ain't no trouble at all. Thanks tho Unc." Lil L slapped me up and I headed back to my car. The grip I had on the envelope turned my knuckles white.

As told by Malcolm

Pablo hit me up saying he had some information for me. When he came to the crib, Essence led him to my office.

"Thanks baby." I thanked her.

"Of course."

"What's good, P?" I slapped Pablo up with my strong arm.

"How you feeling?" he asked.

"I can't complain, I'm just thankful for life."

"I hear that. So look I got what you asked for." Pablo reached into his pocket and handed me an envelope.

"I knew I could count on you." I smiled staring at the envelope I possessed, ready to dig into Latifah's information.

"Anything for you fam. You helped me out a lot."

"It was nothing." I spoke humbly.

"Nah man. It was everything. Sharonda thanks you too man."

"Give Sharonda my love, and those beautiful babies."

"You up next, I seen that fine thing you got up in here."

As told by Essence

"Aye, watch yo mouth fool." Malcolm laughed at Pablo's remark. I probably shouldn't be eavesdropping on Malcolm's conversation, but I couldn't help myself. He could possibly have information regarding Howard. Malcolm wouldn't tell me either way, out of "protection", so I was going to listen in for myself.

"What's up with this Latifah chick anyway?" Pablo asked. I almost threw up my lunch hearing Pablo say her name. I haven't talked to her since the whole thing went down a few weeks ago. She hasn't returned any of my phone calls and I haven't seen her at work. Why was Malcolm asking for information on Latifah? Did he know about us? Oh my God. My hands started to shake uncontrollably as I tried to listen for Malcolm's response.

Ding! Dong! Dammit, who was at the door? I tried my best to get myself together. Whoever it was, it better be good, interrupting my spy work.

"Hey sis." It was Terrance on the other side.

"Hey." I answered flatly.

"Uh, everything good with you?"

"Yeah, I'm good. You?" I really didn't care anything about Terrance's wellbeing at this point, but I didn't want to be rude.

"I'm Gucci, is uh Malcolm here."

"Yes, he's in his office." Terrance proceeded to walk through the foyer.

"Terrance, take off them damn boots." I scowled at him.

He laughed, "There go my sis." Terrance backed up and stepped out his Butta timbs. He mouths "Sorry" to me before heading to the back where Malcolm's office was.

As told by Terrance

I heard another voice besides Malcolm's when I reached the door, so I knocked.

"Come in." Malcolm answered. I walked in to find Pablo in there with him.

"What's good boy." I slapped Pablo up. I haven't seen him in a good minute. It was nice to see he was still holding it down.

"Wassup T." He returned the love.

"Coolin'. Coolin.' You know how I

do."

"Yeah, I know." We all laughed at Pablo's response.

"Look Malcolm, let me know if you need anything else."

"Bet." Malcolm stood up to walk Pablo out.

"Nice seeing you T. We gotta link."

"Hit me," I nodded. I sat in a chair across from Malcolm's desk and waited for him to come back.

"Damn man, where you find that nigga?" I questioned.

Malcolm laughed putting away an envelope that sat on his desk, "just checking up on ya boy. What's good with you tho? Poppin' up to a nigga's house unannounced, ain't like you." Malcolm wasn't being totally honest with me, but whatever. I had things to get off my chest.

I reached into my coat pocket and dropped the envelope Lil L just gave me.

Malcolm's eyes lit up.

"Is that what I think it is?" I nodded my head, "hell yeah" and pushed it over to him to open.

"I haven't looked in it yet. I came straight here after he gave it to me. I wanted you to do the honors." We both smiled.

I was ready to see who was behind all this bullshit, so we can set a plan and execute them. Beads of sweat formed on my forehead as I watched Malcolm tear open the envelope. It was like he was moving in slow motion.

As told by Malcolm

My palms started sweating as I struggled to hold the letter opener up to unseal the envelope. I reached inside to pull out the content. My eyes grew wide at what I read inside.

"What it say?" Terrance asked, but I couldn't answer. I shoved the paper to him, so he can read it himself. I leaned back in the chair trying to retain this information.

Terrance picked up the paper and started reading. He balled up the paper and shot it across the room.

"Hell nah, man," he spoke. I continued to sit quietly.

"This nigga gotta die." Terrance stood up, pacing the floor. I still had no words. The only question I had was why?

"Let's go."

As told by Essence

I strained to listen to Malcolm and Terrance's conversation. Malcolm didn't tell Terrance the real reason Pablo was there. He was doing more than checking on him. Pablo had just given Malcolm information on Latifah. Terrance must've told him about seeing me leave her crib, he was already suspecting her of hitting on me. Fuck. Now what?

Then to top it off, Terrance just delivered more news. This was all too much for me to take. I wonder why Malcolm hid these types of things from me. My stomach began to turn as it tied into knots.

"Let's go." Malcolm broke his long silence. I ran into the bathroom. Last thing I needed was Malcolm to find out I was listening to his conversation.

As soon as I reached the bathroom my head was in the toilet. Everything I had for lunch came out.

"Essence, you okay?" Malcolm ran in and kneeled to my side.

I nodded yes, "I'm okay. It must've been the food we ate." I lied.

"We got to run out real quick. You sure you going to be okay?"

"I'll be fine Malcolm, but are you sure you should be going out. It's only been 2 weeks since you left the hospital. The nurses said you should…"

"Essence, I'm fine. Don't worry." It was hard not to worry.

"I'm sorry."

"Don't be sorry baby. Go get some rest. I'll see you in a bit."

"Take care, sis," Terrance yelled behind him as they both walked out the door.

I watched Malcolm get into Terrance's car and they drove off. I ran back to Malcolm's office to find any information I could. It wasn't like me to be going through his things, but I had to find out some way or another.

On top of his desk was an empty envelope, but I didn't see any paper around the desk that could've come out of it. I tugged at the drawers of his desk, but they were all locked.

"Shit!" I cursed out loud, biting my nails as I scoped out the room, thinking of where it could be. My eyes finally fixated on a balled-up piece of paper in the corner of the room.

My legs wobbled as I walked over to the paper to pick it up. I straightened out the paper to read what the bold red letters said.

"Baby, I forgot something," I heard Malcolm yell up to me. I balled the paper back up, setting it where I found it and ran into the closet. I could feel him inching closer to his office door.

I peeked through the cracks in the closet door and watched Malcolm search the floor. He finally found what he was looking for, the crumbled-up piece of paper I had just discovered. I waited until I was sure the coast was clear before emerging from the closet.

Damn, I didn't get a good look at the paper. All I saw was the name Walter Sutton Jr. I thought long and hard about the name, but it didn't ring a bell for me.

CHAPTER 12

As told by Malcolm

Boom! Boom! Boom! Boom! Boom!
Terrance banged on the door.

"Who the fuck is it?"

Boom! Boom! Boom! Boom! Boom! He banged again.

"I said, who the fuck?" Walt's tough guy voice he had just seconds ago faded when he saw who was behind the door.

"Hey, uh. Sorry bout that. Ya'll was knocking like ya'll was the police or something." Walt laughed nervously, but neither one of us moved a muscle.

"So, what do I owe you for this visit?"

"Your fucking life." Terrance grabbed Walt by his neck and carried him into his living room. I closed the door behind us, making sure no one saw what just went down. Last thing we needed was one of his cracker neighbors calling the police.

Walt fought Terrance's grip, scratching at his hand.

"The more you fight the worse it gets." Terrance teased before letting go. Walt fell to his knees, gasping for air.

"Yo…man…What…the…fuck?" Walt said barely catching wind.

"You tell us what the fuck nigga."

"I…don't…know…what you…mean." Walt continued to find air as he massaged his neck.

"This ring a bell?" I shot the cigar with HLC written on it at him.

His eyes widened up, knowing he had fucked up.

"Oh, you thought we wasn't going to find out it didn't you? You were smart stealing the old bitch car, but you weren't smart enough." Terrance got into his face.

"But we know this wasn't your idea. All you have to do is tell us who paid you." I chimed in.

"Look man, I don't know." Terrance hit him with a jab to his right ribs. I winced at the sight.

"You don't know what?" Terrance asked, now hitting him on the left side.

"Agghhh man. Fuck!" Walt screamed.

"Who sent you to kill me?" It was my turn to speak.

"Gennie, man her name was Gennie." We looked at each other in disbelief. I knew that bitch was too good to be true. Ain't no way she was going to let us off that easy after killing her husband.

"Where she at?"

Walt was now crying uncontrollably.

"Answer him mutherfucker." Terrance kicked the breath out of Walt.

"I don't know man," he gasped. Terrance lifted his foot to imprint his boot on his face. Walt put his arms up in defense. "Look man, I am telling the truth. She had some dudes throw me in the back of a van one day and started pressing me."

"How the fuck she know you know of us?" I wondered.

"Look man, I don't know."

Terrance stepped on his ankle, "Wrong fucking answer."

"Agghhh!" He screamed out.

"You ready to stop bullshitting us?" Terrance asked. Walt nodded his head. Terrance applied more pressure to his ankle before letting up.

"They had to be watching ya'll man. That day I left Jones Place is when they scooped me up. I wasn't tryna kill you man." He turned to me and pleaded.

"Shut the fuck up." Terrance answered for me. Everything he just said hit me hard.

As told by Terrance

I couldn't wait for the opportunity to fuck Walt up. Once a bitch ass nigga, always a bitch ass nigga. All the anger I had built up, he was the lucky recipient. Gennie wasn't playing fair, using this nigga to get back at Malcolm. The bitch moved to Germany for sure, there wasn't no doubt in my mind that she didn't, but she was back.

"Terrance, let me talk to you for a minute." Malcolm snapped me out of my thoughts, saving Walt's life.

I walked over to him to hear what he had to say.

"I don't know what this bitch wants, but we gotta find out ASAP."

"Facts. I can't believe this bitch."

"I can." Malcolm stated coldly.

"It's on you."

Pow! I could see Walt from my

peripheral finding the strength to get off the floor and point his gun at us. He was too slow though. I caught him before his finger reached the trigger.

"Fuck boy." I smirked, watching his body lay lifelessly. One shot to the dome. Without saying one word to each other, Malcolm slid on his leather gloves and we began to destroy the house before sneaking out the door. I sped off Walt's street, hoping no one saw us there.

"Let's find that bitch." Malcolm broke the silence.

"Give me a couple days." I answered. I put a call in and all we had left to do was wait.

As told by Essence

Malcolm came home with a long face. Something was bothering him.

"Baby, what's the matter?"

"I found out who was trying to kill me."

"What?" I was shocked at how blatant he was about it.

"Don't worry baby."

"How can I not worry Malcolm. There is someone out there trying to kill you. They have ties with Howard. We have ties to Howard and I shouldn't be worried?"

"No, you shouldn't be. Because I got this handled."

"Malcolm." I examined his eyes for a different response, but he was adamant. The very thing that turned me on about him, made me so angry at the same time.

"I got you baby, I got us." Malcolm kissed me passionately. My mind was fixated on too many things, to enjoy his kiss. Someone was definitely out to kill him. He was requesting information on Latifah.

As told by Malcolm
As promised, Terrance came through

with the information I needed to find Gennie.

"I knew you'd be calling soon." Her thick accent poured into the phone.

I became angry at her tone, "What's this all about?"

"Relax, Malcolm."

"Relax? Relax? You sent a nigga to kill me and you telling me to relax?" I was a spitting ball of fire, the nerve of her.

"It wasn't my intention to kill you. If it was, you'd be dead. I just wanted your attention, that's all."

What the fuck she mean, she wasn't trying to kill me? I damn near died behind the wheel twice. "Now, you got it. What's up?" I was curious to know what she needed.

"I don't understand why Howard didn't like you. I love your gutta mentality."

"Cut the small talk Gennie, what's up?" I wasn't in the mood for any of her games. She played enough with me.

"I need your help." I stayed silent, waiting for her to continue. "I have a little issue I know you can help me out with."

"What's that?"

"It's a guy I need you to help me take down." Gennie had enough power, I didn't understand why she needed me.

"Look Gennie, I ain't into this shit. Find somebody else, iight?"

"You nigger, you killed my husband. You owe me." In some odd twisted way, Gennie was right. As long as she was alive, she had that shit to hang over my head.

"Fuck." Gennie laughed at me, realizing she had me where she wanted me to be.

"My niece is missing and I need you to bring her back to me, in one piece."

"What the fuck do I look like?"

Ignoring my question, she continued,

"She ran away from Germany to the states. Last time I talked to her, she was working for some guy at a club called Stone."

"Stone?" I asked.

"Yes, sound familiar?"

"Yeah, yeah. I know where that is. If you know where she at, then why don't you just go get her?"

"It's not as easy as you're making it seem. She's been brainwashed."

"Brainwashed?" I laughed, if she only knew how stupid she sounded.

"This is not a laughing matter, I've been watching her. She's been doing drugs. She is not herself."

"What am I going to do about it?"

"I know where to find her boss. He is notorious for taking innocent girls and turning them into his obedient slaves. I need you as back up."

"You don't need me."

"Malcolm, please." I could hear the

desperation in her voice. "Please."

"Iight Gennie, I'm in."

"Ohhh, Malcolm. Thank you so much. I will send over the details."

"Iight."

"Malcolm?"

"What?"

"Leave Terrance out of this, he's too much of a hot head. Poor Walt." She stated before hanging up the phone.

"*Poor Walt.*" What the fuck do she mean, poor Walt? Oh shit! This bitch. She must was there the other day, another thing to hang over our heads. This bitch had to go.

CHAPTER 13

As told by Essence

"Hey, Latifah. It's me...again. Just let me know you're okay. I'm worried about you." I left yet another voicemail on Latifah's phone. Her phone went straight to voicemail each time I called. I even called from the office phone and the same thing.

She still hasn't been back to work. I stared out at her empty desk and reminisced on our blissful morning. What if Malcolm knew about what happened and got her killed? I didn't want to think the worst, but at this point I didn't know what else to think. It all makes sense, I haven't heard from her since Pablo left our house that day to hand off information to Malcolm regarding Latifah.

Walter Summons Jr., the name on the piece of paper I found in his office. I logged into my computer to search his name. I didn't have any swift friends like Malcolm and Terrance to find things out for me. I was determined to find out shit on my own. If Malcolm didn't want to tell me, I would find a way. Walter Summons Jr. was connected to Latifah, somehow, some way.

My search came up empty. Just as I was about to give up, a picture of Jones Place popped up. I read through the county file and found that Walter Summons Jr was the owner of Jones Place. So Walter was the dude giving Malcolm a hard time about buying Jones Place. Now I was confused. I couldn't find a correlation between the two.

I spent the rest of the morning trying to figure out a connection, nothing made sense. I plotted out reasons, but they were all irrational. I needed to talk to Latifah.

"He's making me lose out on money and I don't fucking like it." I heard Vincent talking on the phone. I have never heard Vincent curse, let alone raise his voice. He was always happy.

I knocked on his office door. " I gotta call you right back." He rushed off the phone before calling to tell me to come in.

"Essence." His attitude changed from just moments before, he was the Vincent that I always knew.

"Hey, uh. I was just wondering, uh. Have you talked to Latifah?"

"Latifah, is uh. Out of town working. Can I uh, help you with something?" He fumbled.

"No, uh. It can wait. Do you know when she will be back?"

Vincent's forehead filled with wrinkles as he looked down at his watch, "She should be back this Friday. You sure I can't help you with anything?"

"Yeah. Yeah. I'm sure. Thanks Vincent."

"No problem." Vincent smiled at me and I returned a side smile and headed out.

"Essence?"

"Yes?" I stopped without turning around.

"Shut my door please." I continued to walk out, closing the door behind me.

Latifah, out of town? For some odd reason, I didn't believe Vincent. Why wouldn't Latifah tell me she was going out of town?

"Hey, Frank." I stopped by Frank's desk on the way back to my office.

"Yes mamacita?" Frank answered.

"You talked to Latifah, lately?" I questioned him.

"I have not," he smiled.

"What you looking at me like that for?" Frank was making me nervous.

Frank shoveled through the papers on his desk, "No reason."

"Frank!" I slammed my hand on his desk, causing people to stare at us.

"Chill out, Mama. You're making a scene."

"I'm sorry Frank." I apologized.

Frank rolled his eyes at me, "Look, it's obvious she got to you." I was taken back by what Frank said.

"Wipe the act Essence, Latifah gets all the women in here. Glad I like men because it wouldn't be anything left for me."

"You don't know what you're talking about." I brushed him off.

"I may not know details, but I know how Latifah gets down. She turn ya'll out and have ya'll walking around here looking stupid."

I was shocked.

"Yes, you've been moping around here for weeks since she's been out."

"Frank, I can explain."

"No need to explain to me, I'm not Malcolm." Frank hit a nerve with that one. I loved how honest he was when I first met him, but it's different when you're on the receiving end of things.

"She'll be back. Don't worry." Frank went back to doing his work as if I wasn't still standing there.

I had nothing else to say. Frank was right. Latifah had me stuck on stupid. I walked back to my office with tears in my eyes. Latifah was bringing out a person in me that I didn't know was there, and it wasn't in a good way. She had me dreaming about her, day in and day out. It was supposed to be a secret but if Frank knew there was no telling who else knew. *"She turns ya'll out and have ya'll walking around here looking stupid."* Who was the "ya'll" he was referring to? Was I just another target for Latifah? No. I couldn't be. What we shared was unexplainable.

"I'm not Malcolm." Frank's statements were shooting through my body like sharp pains. What if this got out to Malcolm. How was I going to explain this to him? What about Terrance? He would be devastated too, after all, Latifah was his girl.

"Hey, sis everything good?" I regretted calling Terrance as soon as he picked up. "Sis?"

"Yeah, hey. I'm here."

"You good? Malcolm alright?" Terrance asked.

"He's good. I just was wondering if you heard from Latifah? I got a project at work I need her to help me with and she hasn't been to work. She's not answering her phone either."

"Oh, nah. Last time I talked to her, she said she had to go away for a while to handle some business." Maybe Vincent was telling the truth, maybe she really was out of town.

A feeling of relief relaxed my body.

"Oh okay. Thanks bro."

"Always sis."

As told by Terrance

I can't believe this bitch had Essence searching for her. I was disappointed, but I didn't blame her. Latifah was taking advantage of her.

"Love you." Essence said.

"Love you too sis. Say hey to Malcolm for me."

"I will." Essence hung up.

"You bitch."

"Nigga what?" Latifah shot me a look.

"That was Essence calling." I explained.

"What she say?" Latifah sat up in the

bed with all her attention on me. She acted as if she really fucked with Essence.

"Stop, the act. You were using her."

"Using her? Using her for what?"

"I don't fucking know. You and that bitch ass nigga Vincent."

"Vincent? He has no idea about Essence and I." Latifah tried to convince me.

"Ain't no you and Essence."

"I love her Terrance, I really do." I couldn't help but laugh. Latifah was putting on a good act. She even started crying. If I didn't know the type of snake she was, I would've believed her. Anyone else would have believed her, obviously Essence was falling for it.

"Enough of that. Let's talk about this nigga Vincent."

"What about him?" She sniffed, wiping her nose with her hand.

"Bitch, don't act stupid. We gonna set this nigga up."

"Oh no, Terrance. I can't do that. I did what you asked me to do, I stayed away from Essence. I can't help you take out Vincent."

"You can and you will. Do you need a reminder?" I walked closer to her, prepared to remind her what I was capable of.

"Terrance, leave my family out of this," she pleaded.

I laughed, "Fuck your family, you tried to destroy mine."

Latifah bowed her head, she knew I was right.

"Now, boom here's the plan."

Latifah nodded her head as I gave her a rundown of what was about to go down. I rubbed my hands together, prepared to take care of Vincent. I had a special surprise for Latifah too.

As told by Malcolm

I constantly checked my phone

waiting for Gennie to text me the information I needed. I was ready to help her get her niece back and get my life back in order. I laid in bed with my eyes wide open since I couldn't sleep. I turned to Essence and watched her sleep. She looked so peaceful in her sleep. I kissed her forehead and rolled out of bed.

I went to the fridge and cracked open a beer and headed to my office. The envelope from Terrance still sat on top of my desk, it then reminded me of the envelope Pablo gave me. I unlocked the desk drawer and reached for the envelope.

Gennie resurfacing took my mind off the fact that I even had this information. I didn't bother to use the letter opener to tear into the envelope. I opened it up and read.

Latifah Washington formally known as Farah Landeau; Born August 12, 1977 in Port-au-Prince,

Haiti. Daughter of Beatrice and Makenson Landeau. Farah fled to the United States after killing her father, Makenson, who allegedly raped Farah, and impregnated her in 1997.

Farah settled into Chicago changing her name to Latifah Washington. Shortly after giving birth to her baby boy, Messiah Washington she admitted him into a group home, because she didn't have the means to take care of him in the condition he was in.

Latifah currently works as an administrative assistant at Jackson & Jackson, owned by Vincent Shapiro. Vincent took Latifah under his wing, making sure her and Messiah are well taken care of.

I sat the paper down, in disbelief. This information didn't help me out at all, but it was fucked up.

Buzz. Buzz. I felt my phone vibrate in

my pocket. I had a text message from a blocked number.

EVERYTHING IS A GO, MEET ME AT STONE TOMORROW NIGHT AT 10.

It was Gennie. I picked up the phone to dial Terrance's number, but I decided against it. Gennie was firm about not getting him involved, so wasn't no telling what she may do if she found out I went against her wishes.

I locked the paper up in the drawer, it wasn't relevant at this moment. Essence was still sleeping when I reached our bedroom. I snuggled up behind her and kissed her neck.

"Everything okay?" She whispered.

"It will be." I whispered back with confidence because after tomorrow, everything would be.

CHAPTER 14

As told by Terrance

I hopped out of bed and showered early as fuck this morning. My adrenaline was pumping through my veins like steroids. I was whistling songs and shit while making breakfast. I wasn't an early bird, but today was judgement day. I couldn't wait to see the look on Vincent's face when I slashed his fucking neck.

White boy thought he was tough, but he ain't seen nothing yet. Latifah too. She thought she was off the hook because she stopped fucking with Essence, but I had something for her ass too. She was riding by my Ma Dukes crib, plotting to take her down. Using her as bait to get me to do this bullshit for them. I have to admit, she had me at first. Once I found her weakness it was easy. Messiah Washington. I made a trip up to his residence and took a selfie with him. His condition was fucked up, I didn't want to hurt him, he was already suffering, but I had to make sure Latifah thought I did. I stayed up there and played with him for a little while. He was a smart kid, granted his disease. Not to mention he was innocent, born to a fucked up mother. My young boys said some shit bout her being fucked by her dad, that's why he was fucked up like that. I don't know how true it was, but regardless of the fact. You fuck with mine, I fuck with yours.

"Let's go." I called out to Latifah. She was taking forever to get ready.

"I'm coming nigga, damn." She yelled back. She was a little pit of fire, still. She walked down the stairs dressed in a black jumpsuit. This bitch loved jumpsuits. She knew she was fine as fuck in them.

"Damn, you don't look like you got a 20 year-old. Without thinking, Latifah smacked me across my face.

"Don't you ever mention my son again." I laughed at her as I rubbed my face. She could have that one, she was unknowingly counting down the minutes to her death bed, anyway. Might as well let her enjoy them.

Latifah grabbed her purse off the couch and headed out the side door. I followed behind her, my eyes glued to her little plump ass. We parked down the street from Stone and walked around back.

As told by Malcolm

I needed something to pass by the day

so I decided to go into the office and handle some work. I tried my best to remain focused at Hill Homes, but a lot of shit was being neglected due to my personal life. It was almost over though, I smiled at the thought.

"What you smiling at nigga?" Terrance caught me.

"Nothing," embarrassed that he just caught me.

"A smile like that, it gotta be more than something. Lil' sis, putting it on you like that?" He clowned.

"What I tell you bout that?" I pointed my finger at him, laughing.

He put his hands up as to say don't shoot.

"What you got going on today?" He asked.

"Playing catch up, man. I've been slipping lately."

"Tell me about it, you see that pile over there on my desk?" Terrance pointed to the folders tacked up on his desk.

"What we doing man?" I was serious.

Terrance shook his head, "I don't know man. You ever talk to Gennie?"

"Yeah, but the bitch giving me the run around. Talkin' bout she just wanted to say hi." I lied.

Terrance laughed, "That fine bitch crazy." Terrance was right, she was a crazy bitch. This was the perfect time to let him in on what I knew, but I kept it to myself.

"What you getting into tonight?" I asked him, switching the subject.

"Nothing much,"

"Iight, Imma hit you in the morning. I'm bout to head over to Jones Place before I go home."

"Cool." Terrance responded. He went back to his desk and started sorting through everything.

I drove to Jones Place and parked.

Flashbacks of me first meeting Terrance jogged my memory. I laughed, those kids was ready to whoop my ass. I thought about all the niggas we robbed, all the houses we hit up, and watching the police cuff Terrance and send him away. We had come a long way. Watching the men working on Jones Place proved it, but we were slowly getting pulled back into the bullshit. Once a project kid, always a project kid.

I braced myself for what was about to go down. I searched around the parking lot for any signs of Gennie, but I didn't see any cars. I hope I wasn't walking into a trap. I reached for my phone to call Terrance. I should've been let him know what was going down. Better late than never, I thought. I dialed his number, but he sent me to voicemail. I turned off my phone and went inside.

As told by Essence

"Hey, baby. I got some business to take care of tonight."

"Business?" I asked to clarify.

Malcolm grabbed my hands, "Baby look, when I get home, I will fill you in."

"You promise?"

"I promise." Malcolm stepped away from me and got dressed. He put on a black suit, cufflinks included. He really meant business.

"I love you Malcolm."

"I love you more, Essence." I walked Malcolm to the door, and kissed him as he left. The right thing for me to do was to go upstairs and wait for his return, but I wasn't into doing the right things as of lately. I put on my coat, waiting for Malcolm to pull out the driveway before getting into the car and following him down the street. I followed close enough behind Malcolm to make sure I didn't miss a turn, but far enough not to get caught.

Malcolm finally stopped as he pulled into the parking lot at Stone. What the hell was he doing here?

CHAPTER 15

As told by Terrance

"Latifah, my favorite girl." Vincent stood up and greeted her with a hug.

Vincent finally looked at me, "Terrance."

"Wassup." I nodded my head at him.

"Someone is in a good mood." Vincent noted. He was right, I wanted to stay as calm as I could, for as long as I could. I needed him to be relaxed so he wouldn't see it coming.

I watched Latifah and Vincent chop it up for a second. Latifah was working this nigga, just as she worked me. He knew her longer than I did and he was still falling for it.

"I have to use the bathroom. I'll be right back." That was my cue.

"Hurry back, we got business to discuss." Vincent ordered.

"So, Terrance, my pal. How's life treating you?' He tried to spark conversation.

"Life's great. It'll be better after I..." I reached into my pocket to grab my gun, but was interrupted by a familiar voice.

"Vincent, it's a pleasure to meet you."

It was crazy ass Gennie. I couldn't believe my eyes. I felt my phone vibrate in my pocket, I meant to turn the shit off. I looked at the caller ID, it was Malcolm. I sent him to voicemail and went back to what was in front of me.

"I'm sorry? I don't think we've met."

"No, we haven't met, but I know you. And him. Hey, handsome." She purred at me. I looked at Vincent who was now white as a sheet.

"Nigger, you trying to set me up."

"I don't know what the fuck you talking 'bout." Yes, I did set him up, but it ain't have shit to do with Gennie. I was just as surprised to see her as he was.

"What's this setting up mess you boys talking about. I came to get my niece."

Vincent laughed nervously, "Your niece? I don't know your niece."

Gennie pulled out a picture and set it on the table between us. Vincent's eyes gave it away that he knew exactly who Gennie was talking about. I took a glance at the chick and she looked familiar. She was one of the bitches dressed in all white at the New Year's Eve party Latifah invited me to. Speaking of Latifah, her ass should've been back from the bathroom by now. I was getting a little nervous, but I didn't let it show.

"Just let me take her back to Germany and this will all be over with."

"I told you I don't have your niece."

"You may want to rethink that." Gennie smiled at him.

As told by Malcolm

Soon as I stepped into the back of the club, I heard my cue and busted through the door with my guns drawn. There was two guns pointing back at me. What the fuck? Gennie set me up. I was a damn fool to believe her. Then, I realized who was behind the guns. Vincent and Terrance.

"Malcolm, what the fuck you doing here?" Terrance yelled at me.

"What the fuck you doing here nigga?" I asked back before we both turned our guns on Vincent, who had already grabbed Gennie and had his gun to her head.

"Make one move and this bitch is dead." Terrance and I looked at each other confused as fuck. We could get into the fact that we were both standing here trying to figure out why one another was here, but first we had to take care of this shit at hand.

"Vincent, please. I just want my niece. Give me my niece that's all." Gennie begged. I never saw her so vulnerable. She barely shed a tear about Howard's death. It was clear she wasn't trying to set me up.

"Drop the fucking guns." Latifah's voice was forceful standing behind us. She was holding a gun to both of our necks. I lowered my gun and Terrance followed. Vincent was still holding on to Gennie. He smiled, approving Latifah's tactics.

"You bitch." Terrance spoke.

"No, no. That's not nice." Latifah said, sounding like a mother disciplining her toddler.

"Fuck you." He continued to speak. I didn't say a word. I was too busy trying to wrap my head around everything that was going down.

"Malcolm!" I heard Essence shout my name. What the fuck was she doing here? She must've followed me, she was so damn hard headed.

"Malcolm, what's going on?" She was crying. Latifah slowly lowered the guns she had to our necks giving Terrance enough time to put her in a choke hold.

"Latifah, Vincent. What is going on?" Essence searched for answers from anybody who would listen.

"Essence, I'm sorry." Latifah cried out.

"Shut the fuck up." Terrance pressed his gun deeper into her temple.

"Essence, what are you doing here?' I walked over to her.

"I followed you. I knew something wasn't right. I had to find out what was going on. All these secrets are killing me."

Bang! Bang! I ran to tackle Essence to the ground, trying to save her from any bullet that could have potentially came her way. When I looked up. I noticed Vincent laying in a pool full of blood. Terrance still had a grip on Latifah, using her as a shield to duck for cover. Gennie was the only one standing, with blood splattered on her face.

"Lydia!" She screamed as she ran to a girl holding a gun. I noticed the chick as the one serving us at the New Year's Eve party. Now, that I look at her, she resembled Gennie a little bit. Gennie hugged her tight.

I lifted Essence off the ground, "Go to the car now!" I ordered her.

"Malcolm," she pleaded.

"Now." This was not the time for a debate. Essence almost got herself killed. She had no business being here. She did just as I told her to do.

"Malcolm, thank you so much."

Gennie cried out to me.

"Thank you, Gennie." Terrance stepped in, "I had plans to kill that mutherfucker tonight. This one too." He shook Latifah. Her make-up was smeared all over her face.

Gennie and Lydia walked hand-in-hand. As they reached Vincent's body, Lydia gave him a hard kick before walking out of Stone.

"What we gonna do with her?" I asked Terrance, referring to Latifah.

"She got something to tell you." I was confused. What he mean, she got something to tell me?

"Malcolm, I...I...I'm in love with Essence." She cried. I smiled, this wasn't new information. Anyone could see the say she would look at her. The way she called her beautiful. The way she hugged her. I knew she wasn't into Terrance. I saw her staring at us the whole time we were dancing, when they first met. It was only a matter of time before the truth revealed itself.

"That's it?" I said. She nodded her head.

"T, let's go." Terrance screwed his face up, at me. He continued to hold her, staring at me. I nodded for him to let her go. Terrance let her go, throwing her to the ground.

Terrance and I proceeded to walk out the club. Terrance was hesitant, but he walked beside me. I could hear Latifah bawling as we walked away. I stopped suddenly, with a change of heart.

Bang! Now, it was over.

Made in the USA
Columbia, SC
22 August 2017